THE GARDEN GNOME

Kevin Sweeney

Black Rainbows Press

For Mr Marmalade, Wibble, the Ponies Purple &
Pink, Jelly, and Colin the cauliflower.

"Thou shalt not make unto thee any graven image."
The Second Commandment

Coming soon from the same author…

**THE SHOPPING LIST
THE GARDEN GNOME
THE CROP CIRCLE
THE MICROWAVE**

And, exclusively at GODLESS.COM…

**THE LUSTY
THE GLUTTONS
THE SLOTH
THE GREEDY & THE ENVIOUS
THE WRATHFUL
THE PROUD**

ONE

MONDAY

Mr Farmer brought something nasty back with him. He also brought his snaps. He always brought his snaps.

The end of everything began on a spring morning when Rosie Amis stepped out of her house to do some pottering in her garden and found her favourite gnome had returned from his latest bit of globetrotting. He was back in his usual spot, down by Ted's shed with the rhubarb she was forcing, standing between the upturned buckets in which she had punched holes for daylight to slip through; growing rhubarb in the dark, with only minimal light to strive upwards for, made for a much paler, extremely sweet tasting flesh. It had always been Ted's favourite dessert, rhubarb crumble, as well as the source of his favourite joke, which he had never failed to tell his wife whenever she served up the first of the year's crop.

"You see Rosie old girl, this little boy was watching a man shovelling up manure in the road, from the rag and bone man's carthorse, you see, and the boy asks the man what he wants a load of horse poo for? And the man says, I'm going to put it on my rhubarb... and the boy says, he says, at my house we put custard on ours!"

And he'd roar with laughter and she'd smile like she didn't hear that joke every year for nearly four decades of marriage.

Looking at Mr Farmer with his book of snaps leaning against her forcing buckets, the pain from losing Ted ripped through her again, as fresh as if he'd died yesterday, and not nearly five years before.

Mr Farmer had started taking his trips not long after. Ted passed. Rosie wasn't so dotty that she didn't know the connection; in the working man's club that they'd held the wake in, where Ted had spent every Friday night for many, many years, she remembered voicing the one regret she had in her life to one of the neighbours, Mr Flemming from two doors down. All of the neighbours had turned up, because Rosie and Ted were well known and well liked. But Mr Flemming was the one she had been speaking to when she was just tiddly enough and maudlin to voice her secret.

"We never saw the world! Ted was happy with Cornwall, year after year, every year. He said you didn't need to go to those foreign places where you didn't know what you'd be eating for your breakfast, not when Cornwall was only a few hours away... I tried suggesting all sorts of things, short breaks, packages, a bit of touring, maybe even a cruise... but no, my Ted was nothing if not set in his ways..."

It really was her only regret, not travelling. There was no reason they shouldn't have. They had never had children, but that was something they'd both agreed on; she had felt no mothering instinct, ever, and Ted said the world was only getting worse, and if it was getting worse, why curse another generation?

They joked -or at least, Ted did- that the garden gnomes they acquired over the years were their children.

But she'd always wanted to see a bit more of the world, before it nuked itself, or the air wasn't breathable anymore and the oceans were sterile.

Mr Flemming had been a little taken aback by her bleak attitude, but then, he'd had two boys, so he would. But the Amis's were well liked in their street, and so four months after the funeral, Mr Farmer had gone missing from her garden. She'd wondered at the time why a thief would steal just the one gnome, particularly when there were a devil's dozen of her children dotted around the cheerful chaos of growing veg and flowers, but then a few days later he was back in the rhubarb patch... and he had an album of photographs with him.

That was the first set of holiday snaps.

Mr Farmer had been to Dublin for the weekend.

There were snaps of the ruddy cheeked concrete gnome taken with pints of Guinness, including one in the gravity bar at St James Gate brewery. There were snaps of him taken with stag parties dressed in drag in Temple Bar. There were snaps of him taken with a statue of Molly Malone, and snaps of him below the bullet holes in the wall of the Grafton Street Post Office.

Rosie had been delighted, and the first thing she had done was head around to the Flemming's, because she knew Mr Flemming often had business over in Ireland, and maybe he could tell her if he recognised the locations in the pictures...? And it was Mr Flemming who had put a name to the places that the cheerful gnome had visited.

After that, Mr Farmer became a regular jet-setter.

Two to three times a year the gnome would vanish from his place among the rhubarb, only to reappear a week or a fortnight later, always with a slim album of photographs documenting his trips. At some point he had taken to writing down what he was doing and where he was on the backs of the pictures, and even though his handwriting tended to change from trip to trip... the writing style was a lot like how her Ted would talk, including terrible puns and jokes.

Just like her Ted, it seemed Mr Farmer was a cheeky devil, a regular Jack-the lad!

He went to St Lucia one Summer, around about the same time as the Bronte's at number forty-five had for their twentieth wedding anniversary, though they said they hadn't bumped into him. When the Krishnamurthi's on the corner had gone to Pakistan for a cousin's wedding, the gnome had apparently smuggled himself in their luggage, and Rosie was delighted to see him treated the same as every other guest at the lavish ceremony.

Mr Farmer visited Thailand after the Walker's divorced; it had been surreal to see him being adored by so many go-go dancers in various Bangkok nightclubs. He visited Germany, which was apparently his ancestral home. He went to Providence, Rhode Island, USA, and paid his respects at the grave of a writer called Lovecraft.

Ted had spoken up in her mind once on the matter, and called Mr Farmer "their prodigal son."

Rosie left the gnome be whilst she did her bit of pottering. She worked until she was too tired to do anymore -which was a shorter and shorter time every month, it seemed- and then she collected up her few tools and the album of snaps and plodded back inside.

Halfway back to the house she realised she had forgotten her hand-fork. It was still stuck in the rosemary tub.

Well, it could stay there. She needed a cuppa, and she was eager to see where Mr Farmer had been for the past two weeks. Maybe he had hitched a lift with the Wirral's when they had gone over to Egypt...

*****

and here i am with my mate the spinks!!! heain't got a nose, so how does he smell??? terrible!!!

It was a very clever shot, using forced perspective to make it look like Mr Farmer was huge and standing between the paws of the world famous monument, whose name he had misspelled.

Rosie had enjoyed his tour around the five star hotel he was staying in, marvelling at the grandeur she would only ever know at second-hand, narrated by Mr Farmer's bad jokes and worse puns. Then Mr Farmer had decided to hit the tourist spots.

good spot to soak up some sun!!! a "giza" wants to look his best!!!

Another clever shot; it looked like the gnome was colossal, and was lying back on one slope of a pyramid, as if he were actually sunbathing. It took her a moment to figure out the joke; geezer, Giza...

Rosie sipped tea, smiling. It was the kind of crap pun Ted would have loved.

The cat flap creaked, and moments later, Cookie her British Short Hair cat hopped up onto the sofa next to her. She stroked him once, down the whole length of his spine, and turned to the next page in the album.

Now Mr Farmer was normal sized again, balanced precariously on the back of a camel.

this bloke really gave me the hump!!!

Rosie groaned and smiled.

The next picture featured a man stood on his own, no Mr Farmer in sight. The man was almost a caricature of the kind of person you would expect to see in Cairo, if your head was stuffed full of offensively clichéd stereotypes and words like *swarthy*. He wasn't smiling.

met this bloke in one of those cafes where they smoke hookers!!! he said he knew a great places to do selfies!!!

The next series of pictures were different to the ones that came before. They started as shots of busy Cairo streets, streets in which a few recognisable places -a KFC, a shop selling football shirts of Premiership teams- gradually diminished. The presence of people thinned out, and the buildings grew older, more neglected. Mr Farmer's comments were as alternately asinine and cheesy as ever, however, which helped to lessen the unease Rosie felt rising in her.

everyone here supports manchester united bloody typical!!!

my new mates name is mohammed which is egyptian for joe bloggs!!!

bit off the beaten track now!!!

mohammed said we we're going to a temple, an old one, REELLY old!!!

i didn't know gods could be forgotten!!!

At some point they went underground. Walls of brick with chaotic electrical wires nailed into them became stone tunnels illuminated by burning braziers.

Mr Farmer turned up in the next photograph. Rosie squinted, trying to make out details, but the poor light made the whole scene seem blurred with smoke. The gnome was in some sort of room, or cave, standing at the feet of three statues. The statues were crude and somehow... *nasty*. Rosie didn't know why she felt that way, and certainly couldn't have pointed to any specific detail, but the word that best fit her emotional reaction was... *nasty*.

The statue on the left was covering its eyes, or trying to dig them out. The one in the middle had its hands over its mouth, or was trying to stop something squirming its way past its lips…

The one on the right had its hands over its ears and it was shrieking in pain or terror.

Rosie shivered.

It looked like that horrible "Scream" painting. She'd always hated that picture, but the statue was worse; as crude as it was, almost like one of those Easter island heads stretched out, the features of its face somehow conveyed a sense of profound terror mixed with despair, as if it had seen that Thing in nightmares which you always wake up before glimpsing its face.

my new mates told me a secret and i can't wait to tell my brothers and sisters!!!

That was the last picture.

Rosie felt very uneasy. Those last pictures weren't like the usual sort of thing Mr Farmer did. Of course she knew it was her neighbours all acting together who took the photographs when they went away, taking her gnome with them, writing the silly little missives... but there was a pattern, a kind of formula that they all must have agreed to, or which had arisen organically over time. And this set of snaps had deviated, with that strange journey to some old shrine beneath the Cairo streets, filled with weird idols.

Rosie suddenly felt a need to talk to the Wirral's.

She looked them up; Norman and Shirley.

She tapped the number into her phone with the oversized buttons, so she didn't need her specs to dial.

She waited a lot longer than she normally would have before she gave up on the ever ringing line.

Rosie sat in her front room and tried to reassure herself. But she couldn't.

She might have been able to tell herself that the Wirral's were out, either gone out to dinner or merely to the back garden for a spot of weeding... except the number she had used was Norman's mobile. And nobody went anywhere without their mobile, especially not Norman, a retired doctor who had not shaken the habit of being on-call.

She heard Ted's voice in her head, as she did quite often these days, his cigar roughened voice speaking plain and simple truths;

Now, now, old girl, what are you spooking for? Some silly snaps of a dusty tourist trap! What's there to it?

Well, there was nothing of course, just vague feelings, no more substantial than broken cobwebs.

The cat flap creaked.

Rosie opened the album to the last picture again, of Mr Farmer standing there with the three idols. They reminded her of something, but whatever it was wouldn't come to the front of her mind, let alone the tip of her tongue.

my new mates told me a secret and i can't wait to tell my brothers and sisters!!!

That was a weird thing to write. What was it supposed to mean? Norman and Shirley Wirral were practical people. Norman might have been playful if he had a few glasses in him -in fact, some years ago, he'd gotten overly playful with Rosie after the better part of a bottle...- but she couldn't see either of them taking Mr Farmer's adventures down such a subtly dark path.

...my new mates told me a secret and i can't wait to tell my brothers and sisters...

Something else nagged at Rosie.

The noise in the kitchen was so quiet that she had been hearing it for a few minutes before she realised it was even there.

A rustling sound?

Rosie suddenly knew what was wrong when Cookie stood up and arched her back, hissing at the sound.

What was wrong was the other sound she had heard a little bit before, the sound of the cat flap creaking... when the cat had never left the sofa.

It wasn't a rustling sound precisely, but it was hard to say exactly what it was. The closest thing she could think was it was like two pieces of very fine sandpiper rubbing against each other, a gritty, sliding sound.

The door to the kitchen was open. If she leaned forward, she would be able to see most of the interior.

But she didn't want to.

Something inside her, something very old, told her that looking inside the kitchen right now would be a very bad idea. It also suggested running, getting out of the house and getting far, far away.

NOW.

Cookie bolted from the room, heading for the hall that lead to the stairs and the front door.

She really should have followed the cat, rather than doing what she did do.

Rosie leaned forward slowly because she did everything slowly nowadays, and she looked in the kitchen.

The sound of rubbing sandpaper was in fact the sound of limbs that should never have been able to move. Legs walking, legs made of sculptured and painted concrete.

Mr Farmer.

The garden gnome.

When he saw her see him, he sped up.

He was carrying the gardening fork she had left behind, though his holding the tool made it look more like a grotesquely proportioned pitchfork.

Rosie heard Ted in her mind. He was doing a very poor impression;

Gerroff my lahhhnnnd!

He was upon her before she even thought of trying to move, raising the garden fork high over his head before stabbing it down hard throughthe top of her foot.

For such a little thing, he was immensely strong. The tines of the fork punched straight through the skinny, liver spotted flesh and bones to emerge through the sole of her slipper and into the boards beneath the carpet .

She shrieked and instinctively tried to jerk her foot away. But she was pinned, and all that did was turn the dial on the pain up another few notches.

Rosie almost passed out. The world turned grey and fuzzy around the edges, and then she felt her eyeballs starting to roll up in her skull, but somehow she fought it.

Her vision swam.

When it came clear again, he was already clambering over her knee, tiny concrete hands grabbing bunches of her faded old M&S sundress to haul himself up. The sandpaper rubbing sound accompanied all his movements, but the only part of him that did not move was his face, his fixed grin gleefully moronic.

Rosie cried out and swatted at him with the back of her hand, terrified panic making her hit him as hard as she could.

Fresh pain exploded as bones broke on his painted concrete features.

This finally was too much for her, and this time the fuzzy grey darkness descended fully.

*****

She was having a sexy dream. It had been a long time since she had had one of those.

In it, her Ted was alive and well, and they were having fun. One finger of his was fumbling at her entrance, awkward as a teenager. The finger was rough and cool.

Rosie felt very, very faint stirrings. She had thought the ashes were dead, but their seemed to be an ember or two amongst them, ready to be sifted, coaxed into heat, ready to ignite if fresh fuel were added.

But she was too dry down there. The sticky days were long over.

She told Ted he needed something, told him to spit in his hand first before he...

The cool, rough thing entered her. Too dry. It hurt.

She told Ted to be careful. She hadn't forgotten how big he was, and if he was serious about this and not just playing silly buggers he needed to grease that huge old donkey dick of his up before he...

He shoved forward. Dry.

It felt like his cock was wrapped in sand paper. Huge and cold and so rough it scraped the delicate tissues of her sex, stinging painfully.

The dream fell away in gauzy folds as her consciousness surfaced, but she was still in pain. Her foot and her hand were dipped in boiling, burning petrol, and her vagina was being scraped by something...

She was still on the sofa. Her sundress had been split, and she could see a tiny back arched between her legs, driving itself forward and into her.

Her brain tried to process the horror of what she was seeing, tried to match it up with what her sixty eight years of sane, reasonable life told her was true about the world, and all it did was belch up some poetry she had been forced to learn as a school girl;

> *"And what rough beast,*
> *Its hour come round at last,*
> *Slouches towards Bethlehem to be born?"*

The garden gnome was crawling up inside her cunt, as if to take the place of the children she had never borne.

The prodigal son.

Rosie screamed, staring down at her sex grown swollen taut and tight and painful with the foot tall, enormously rotund figurine forcing himself in inch by inch. It looked like she had a balloon growing between her thighs, a balloon tufted with fine silvery pubic hair. She grabbed at his legs and tried to pull him out, but she wasn't able to secure a grip, he'd just kick himself free of her fingers and stuff himself in ever deeper.

The lips of her pussy began to split, the skin stretched too far.

A small hand found the opening to her uterus, and began to tug at it, widening it. Ripping her.Going deeper.

Rosie didn't die sane. This was a mercy.

The mercy was granted by a sound.

The creaking of the cat flap.

A creaking which happened not once, not twice, but a dozen times, as more and more of her children followed the prodigal son home.

*****

Many hours later, the old ladies' corpse finally gave way in a grotesque mockery of the miracle of birth, her pelvis snapping like the wishbone from a turkey as her roiling belly split wide and lawn gnomes flooded out of her like fish let loose from a net onto a boat's deck.

Gradually, in ones and in twos, her concrete progeny began to leave the house via the cat flap, each eager to share their secret, venturing out into the world to whisper in senseless ears and coax the inanimate into locomotion. The greater mass of them wandered downhill, towards the nearby industrial estate.

Cookie came back after they were gone. Hungry.

The cat found its owner. Rosie was lying with her head back, mouth and eyes wide open. What was also wide open was her torso from the navel down. After sniffing curiously at the ruin between her owner's thighs, Cookie, without much hesitation, began to eat her pussy.

TWO

FRIDAY - EARLY MORNING

The biggest pain in the arse about working for a sex toy wholesaler was the practical jokes that got played in the office. They got old really fucking fast.

Liam Shardlow's desk was occupied by an inflatable doll.

It was a Lovely Linda, a pretty basic model from the early years of the industry, so old that she was in fact named after Linda Lovelace from the vintage bongo movie *Deep Throat*. They only kept a few of them in stock for the occasional collector who wanted her for her historical significance. Most people who wanted a love-companion these days were used to much more realistic products than the old blow-up models with their hard plastic orifices.

And there she was sat at his desk, or at least, wedged in place by the chair shoved under her, leaving her stiffly tilted backwards. Lovely Linda wasn't poseable, and the most flexibility you could get out of her was letting some air out so she would bend more easily.

Liam turned the kettle on as he passed the tiny kitchenette area that had been shoe horned in at the far end of the limited space; the office was one of those pre-fabricated shoeboxes that pop up on building sites, filled with cheap flat-pack furniture. It was positioned in the far corner of the industrial unit that the company operated out of, the rest of the space filled with racking filled with stock, and a packing and processing area. Even though the company had operated at a profit for the past five years, the owner and managing director hadn't seen fit to re-invest some of that money into a more permanent seeming operation; the whole feel of the place was fly-by-night.

Liam handled imports, but had a feeling that the company was actually a front for something else. Though nothing illegal passed through his hands, he had his suspicions that a lot of the orders were just laundering money made in other "business" ventures.

But he kept his mouth shut. The money was good, the work was more or less stress free if you factored out the vague fear you were part of a criminal organisation, and he liked most of the people he worked with, except for Mr Coolbear.

Even if the same old jokes kept getting recycled...

He pulled his chair back and retrieved Lovely Linda, propping her against the wall whilst he booted up his computer. She made squeaky noises as he handled her, cheap PVC rubbing, a sound a lot like that made by balloons as clowns tied them into animal shapes. As his workstation came to life it informed him that it was about to perform a half dozen different updates, which was fine by Liam as it gave him time to wander back to the kitchen area and prep his first mug of coffee for the day.

There was a tiny square of yellow on Linda's left breast.

He plucked the Post-It note off.

In tiny handwriting, there was a message;

wot a "dolly" this one is!!! she left me breathless!!!

Was that supposed to be joke? Well, that certainly ruled out his office colleagues, as June was actually funny, and Mr Coolbear had the humour of a corpse.

Sod it, coffee time.

Three spoons of instant Nescafe, three spoons of his own jealously guarded ration of demerara sugar, and the milk in first. He gave the milk a sniff first, just to make sure the overnight fuck-up fairies hadn't turned it into yogurt. No, it was still good, though he wished Mr Coolbear would budget them for that filtered stuff that lasted for seven days after you opened it...

Something squeaked, a short and slow sound.

Eh?

Liam turned towards the noise.

The office was still empty. Early bird Liam was still alone.

Except for Lovely Linda, still leaning against the wall, begging for it with her soulless eyes, thick red lips, and tits the shape of mini traffic cones.

What had he heard? It had sounded like... well, it had sounded like someone mucking about with the blow-up doll, but he was alone, and blow-up dolls were inanimate objects that did not move by themselves.

So. He was hearing things.

Huh.

It was just as he started to pour hot water onto the thick paste in the bottom of his mug that June Swann walked in, rattling an umbrella free of rain.

"Mornin' Liam," she called cheerfully. "It's raining cats and dogs out there..."

"I hope you didn't step in a poodle," he said, automatically.

She pretended to strike a drum set, finishing with a cymbal clash.

"Bah-dum, *tsshh!*"

He sighed.

"Oh, hello, that was heartfelt," said June. "Two questions; what's up, and is the milk okay?"

He started making June's mix, which was half a spoon of instant and enough sugar to trigger diabetes.

"Do you think if I put in a request, Coolbear will get us a new joke book?"

June made a face of mock outrage, pretending to be offended.

"Well I am sorry," she said. "But I thought our back and forth routine had transcended rote and achieved the level of a shibboleth."

"What's a shibboleth?"

"A formalised set of words that act as a ritual between contemporary groups acting as a sort of password."

Liam was not shocked by how easily she rattled this definition off. June was scary-smart, the kind of intelligent that made Liam wonder why the hell she was working for Pleasure World Ltd. She was also twelve years his senior, and had two daughters by two separate husbands.

Liam was only a little bit in love with her.

Only a little. Just from the delicate spray of laughter lines at the corners of her eyes to the slightly buck toothed grin that constantly played about that big mouth...

Only a tiny bit in love.

He told himself this, even when his colleague was the basis of eighty percent of his shower-wank fantasies.

"You want to quit our double act, is that it?" she asked.

"No," said Liam. "I meant a new joke book for everyone. There's only so many times you can find an item of stock occupying your work space and still find it funny."

June lifted an eyebrow as she lifted her mug. She sipped her barely-coffee, and looked towards Liam's desk.

"Ahhh," she said eventually. "Me coffee is just how I likes it, and, ahh, now I'm on your wavelength. A Lovely Linda!"

Her rucksack over one shoulder, June carried her drink over to Liam's desk.

"Alrigh'darlin'," she growled at the doll, "get your coat on, you've pulled."

Liam laughed.

"See, I've still got some fresh material," said June. She sipped hot sugar water with a coffee afterthought. "So, who are we betting on, Piotr or Pavel?"

The two senior warehouse operatives were in charge of the evening lock up, with a member of the office staff, normally Liam, in charge of opening up each morning. It stood to reason it would have been one of them.

"I don't know," said Liam. "But they always act as each other's alibi anyway."

June shrugged.

"You're right, it is a bit played out, isn't it? And it's not even as if they've gone to any trouble, like putting a picture of your mum's face over it..."

"Thanks."

"Just let her down gently, eh?"

"Arfarf."

"Liam, my dear, dear Liam, have you never wondered why I keep Steely Dan IV on my desk?"

He glanced towards that object.

The thing called Steely Dan IV was a chromium plated steel dildo of, as the catalogue put it, "macrophallic proportions". It was eighteen inches in length and thick as a forearm, and came with its own specially adapted nine volt battery pack for those who enjoyed electro-stimulation in their BDSM play.

"Paperweight?" Liam guessed.

June shook her head.

"No. This is the 21st century, the time of the paperless office, so you're as wrong as it's possible to be. The truth is, around about the fifth morning I came in to find an artful arrangement of baby Jesus butt plugs laid out across my workstation I selected the most shocking and intimidating item in our catalogue and adopted it as my mascot. Old Steely Dan IV there trumps anything the warehouse boys can cook up."

Liam nodded thoughtfully. Again, he thought about asking where she got the name from, and again he did not; June never flaunted her intelligence, but he had no intention of clearly displaying his ignorance. Not if he could help it, anyway.

Mr Coolbear came in, unwrapping a scarf from around his neck. He folded it with precise neatness, in the same way that the handkerchief sticking up from his jacket pocket was folded with neat and sharp creases, and the thin grey and blonde beard around his mouth was trimmed with equally fastidious neatness.

"Good morning Mr Coolbear," said June and Liam, almost in perfect sync.

"Has that kettle long boiled?" he asked in reply.

"Just a few minutes ago," said Liam, and waited for Mr Coolbear to empty the thing and refill it with fresh cold from the tap, as he did every morning, because he believed you boiled all the oxygen out of it, resulting in a flatter tasting coffee.

Mr Coolbear set out his own bits and pieces for his morning drink, each in order that he would add them to the mug he unwrapped from the paper he had stored it in overnight, then scowled at the blow up doll next to Liam's desk.

"Has someone been playing silly buggers?" he asked, as if it were Liam's fault.

"Yes, but..."

"That is stock. It has been out the wrapper, meaning used. So we cannot sell it now, can we? Against hygiene rules. I suppose someone is going to pay for it, reimburse the company, hmm?"

Shit...

Liam knew he could either he refuse to have his pay garnished for the very fair reason that it was nothing to do with him, earning him a black mark, or he could gain a black mark by paying for it and thereby admitting, in some obscure way, culpability for mucking about.

June tried to rescue him.

"Liam just came in to find her here... you do know it has to be either Piotr or Pavel that actually did it?" she asked.

Mr Coolbear was flapping one hand in irritability as he fixed his drink.

"Peter, Paul, whoever," he said. June bit her lip; the casual racism of rendering the Polish worker's names into English was a pet peeve. "The company does not care so long as it is not out of pocket. Now, do we not we all have work to do?"

Liam and June shared a look.

"And Liam, get that thing out of here pronto," said Mr Coolbear. "Blasted thing gives me the willies."

Nobody chuckled, because Mr Coolbear wasn't trying to make a joke. He never did.

Liam set his coffee down at his desk and picked up the blow up doll. He tucked her under his arm like a surfboard and headed out into the warehouse, watched by a scowling Mr Coolbear and June, who was desperately trying to stifle the giggles.

Out in the warehouse the radio was blaring from overhead speakers, the Friday morning mix of songs designed to get the working stiffs of the country ready for the weekend.

It put a little spring in Liam's step.

TFI and all that.

It was a few minutes off the official start of the working day, which meant Piotr and Pavel would be holding court over in the packaging and despatch area, chatting with the seemingly never-ending and interchangeable groups of "nieces" and "nephews" that they hired on. Liam reckoned, over the past few years, at least seventy percent of the local Polish population had probably worked for Pleasure World, but he had serious doubts as to whether the rotating and changeable staff that the brothers organised according to their own arcane system of management were all actually blood relatives. Not that Liam, or the company, actually cared, as they were all unfailingly hard working and honest, although none of them stayed long enough to become inured to the squeamish laughter some of the more outrageous stock items would provoke amongst the uninitiated.

And there were certainly some outrageous products for sale...

Lovely Linda under his arm, Liam began to negotiate the ranks of tiered racking that held every kind of conceivable sex toy.

There were aisles devoted to dildos, organised according to brand, size, material, and special features. There were aisles for vibrators, similarly organised. Ben waa balls, butt plugs, strap-ons, all had their places, QR coded to a central database. There were aisles of various fetish wear as well, of course, but only of the most generic varieties and sizes, as that part of the market was largely tied up by boutique companies.

And then of course, there were the sex dolls.

If there were one particular area of the adult entertainment accessory marketplace that Pleasure World Ltd could be said to have a speciality in, it would be inanimate companionship. They boasted fake fuck friends to suit every taste and budget, with a stock that was not only ethnically inclusive -there wasn't a race not represented in their on-line catalogue- but which extended into exotic realms most had never dreamed of.

Did the customer have a thing for dwarfs? Pleasure World had dwarf dolls. Did the customer have a thing for multiple amputees? Pleasure World stocked models with detachable limbs just for that taste. How about aliens? Pleasure World had sex dolls modelled after the sinister Greys who secretly control the world, and also knock-off versions of trademarked characters from numerous sci-fi franchises. They had ultra-realistic corpses for the necromantic. They had mermaids, and giants, and clowns. In fact, the only red-line drawn in the catalogue was children, as there you got into some extremely fuzzy legal grounds.

The Lovely Linda under Liam's arm was tame and primitive compared to the rest of the stock. But even for all the bells and whistles and unusually located orifices they might boast, nothing in stock could do what she did next.

With a balloon-animal squeak, she turned her head around one hundred and eighty degrees to look up at Liam.

He caught the movement in his peripheral vision, and he didn't even break his stride when he glanced down to see the doll was looking at him.

He actually kept walking for another five feet before he cried out and threw the thing away from him.

Linda bounced off a shelf of flavoured anal lubricant. They rattled.

Liam stared at Linda as she came to a gentle landing on the grubby concrete floor.

She was lying on her back, arms extended for a hug. With a squealing squeak, her head slowly twisted back around to its proper position.

She sat up.

Liam's mouth was suddenly dry as cotton.

It was then that Piotr appeared, coming around the end of the aisle, his scanner in hand, working on the touch screen with a stylus.

He saw Liam and bellowed heartily;

"Good morning to you, boss Liam! It is a good morning, am I right? Fuck-ingfriday, yeah!"

Liam didn't answer him.

Piotr followed Liam's gaze. He frowned when he saw the doll on the floor.

"What is this? What is happening here?" he asked.

The doll stood up.

"Fuck-ing shit!"

"Yeah," said Liam.

Lovely Linda stood unsteadily. She was such a primitive model her feet didn't have toes, they were just flesh coloured clubs. Similarly, her hands were just paddles, and when she patted them together twice, a double clap like a master summoning a servant, they made a flat, dull sound.

Chop-chop!

This was the signal.

Piotr and Liam stared.

Behind them, all around them, the packaged sex toys on the shelving began to stir.

Small boxes and plastic wrapped packages bounced and jiggled in their places until they fell forwards; the racking was designed to slope downwards, with ball bearing runners that allowed the next item to slide forward after the first had been picked. Stock began to tumble onto the ground, and when it did it burst the seams of whatever packaging it was in, be it neat cardboard sleeves or sealed plastic clamshells.

Fake fuck friends of every variety began to tear their way free of their trappings. Inflatable versions began to swell with air, as if blown up by invisible lungs, whilst fully pose-able models that had been contorted into extreme yoga positions in order to squeeze them into the smallest possible packaging began to unfold themselves.

"What is this!" cried Piotr. He looked at Liam. "Boss Liam, what do we do?"

Liam didn't answer with words.

He simply turned and ran.

Back to the office.

THREE

TUESDAY

After the HR lass had left him alone he locked the door and quickly scanned the room for security cameras, and when he saw there were none he freed his erection with a sigh of relief.

Fucking HELL, the tits on that lass!

And she was going to be first in line for training!

This was too good an opportunity to miss.

The room she had given him to do the training in was the kind of anonymous meeting room that every mid-sized company has, to be booked for performance reviews, product selection, and all the usual meetings that were the bread and butter of middle-management. Corporate art on the wall, a very sorry looking cheese plant in one corner ostensibly there to oxygenate the room, and the table and chairs, pushed up against one wall as he had asked, giving him ample floor space to set out a number of matts for the employees who were designated as the company's First-Aiders.

Travelling from place to place providing training and certification in first aid practice and the

correct use of defibrillators was Cowan Herd's job...
but his weakness was tits.

Big fucking tits.

He set his two cases down in the corner with
the plant, heart fluttering, breathing shallow, and
gripped himself around the root.

Fucking, fucking, fucking HELL!

Sophia Armitage, the HR lass for Caldwell
Solvents Ltd, had the tits of his dreams. He'd
arrived prompt at eight-thirty in reception and she'd
emerged from a door behind the desk almost as
soon as he'd finished signing the visitor book. The
sour faced cow who was running the phones had
smirked at his reaction when Sophia had walked in,
and it was only that smirk, glimpsed from the corner
of his eye, that had prompted him to slap on his
professional smile and look her in the eyes before
she clocked him looking.

The image of the golden crucifix she wore
almost lost between the huge swells of her breasts
was carefully filed away in his memory wank-bank.

They'd made the introductions, gotten the
obligatorycup of tea, and made it to the room she
had set aside all without Cowan leaving his crotch
on view, mainly by his carrying his duffel bag full
of equipment in front of him. The visible distortion
of his trousers was the only thing giving away the
fact that he wanted to bounce her head off the
nearest hard surface and fuck the shit out of her
drooling, unconscious mouth.

For a loving family man with twin daughters
who had just started primary school, Cowan Herd

was subject to incredibly intense, violent daydreams.

His erect cock was twitching with his heartbeat. He had it out in a public place. He could be caught. And he was about to do something incredibly nasty.

Something he had done more than a few times before… but which was still so exciting.

Second-hand degradation.

The adrenaline blasted through him and he wasted no more time.

He dumped the duffel bag on the floor and frantically hauled out the contents. Cowan's job was training company staff in the various first-aid techniques they needed to know by law, and the gear that he tipped on the floor reflected this. Rolled up mats of thin, rubber sheathed foam like giant, blue spring-rolls were chucked to one side, as were a few thin neck pillows, an ambu bag, bandages, plasters, ice-packs, and leaflets full of acronyms designed to help people remember proper treatment procedures, until there, at the bottom, he found what he was looking for and hauled her out.

Resusci Anne was a teaching aid, used for demonstrating and practising cardiopulmonary resuscitation and the Heimlich manoeuvre. Anne was just a beige torso with a beige head attached; her chest had a convincing feel to it of hard plastic ribs with a pair of plastic bellows within. Her face was incomplete, missing from the cheekbones up, but that was not important. Her nose and mouth were the only parts needed for the training exercise, and for Cowan's immediate needs, only the mouth was necessary.

Her thin, hard plastic mouth.

"Hello Sophia," Cowan whispered. "My name's Cowan, I'm from the... I beg your pardon? Yes, I did notice those big fat fucking titties of yours! And yes, this is my cock! Very happy to meet you!"

He was just about to get started when he realised there was writing on her face. Blinded by lust, he had just thought it was some sort of smudge, but now he saw it was words. Someone had written something very small on Resusci Anne's left jaw, just below her moulded plastic ear;

i told her my best knock-knock gag and she never laughed!!! i asked her, can't you take a "choke"???

"What the bloody... Anya," he muttered.

His daughter was always messing around with his work gear, but this was the first time she had ever defaced anything. It stood to reason it had to be her, the hand writing was so small and her twin Cora-Beth was too timid for such tricks. Still, Cowan didn't know how she had come up with such a tasteless pun, but he would be having words with that little madam later.

Right now, he had to be quick.

Not bothering to try and wipe the writing off, seeing as though he was going to need to clean Anne properly in just a few minutes, he gripped his erection in one hand and lifted the teaching device by the back of her head.

He really needed some lube.

He let himself go, spat in his hand. Soon his shaft was glistening like slugs had been crawling all over it.

"Take this, you massive titted cunt," he hissed, and stuffed his cock into the hard plastic mouth.

The actual fantasy wasn't so much him imagining that the PR lass was eagerly gobbling up his inches -he was balding and podgy, he knew his days as Jack-the-Lad were well over- so much as the knowledge that he was going to fuck this thing until he filled its mouth cavity with spunk, and then, in about twenty minutes times, the bitch with the gigantic tits who would never look at him twice if they passed in the street, would be placing her mouth in the place where he had been.

A blow job by the transitive property.Sort of. He'd clean it out, of course, but still... microscopic traces of his spunk would soon be in that massive titted cunt's mouth.

He just loved the nastiness of the thing.

He had to be quick.

Cowan wrapped both hands around the back of Resusci Anne's plastic head and forced her to bob up and down on his cock. It was rough, but he just told himself that she was using her teeth. He closed his eyes and started to tell her in explicit detail all the things he wanted to do to her, particularly her fun-bags; he wanted to slap them, scratch them, bite her nipples, punch them until they turned black...

Apparently, Resusci Anne took this personally, and chomped down on his dick with a wet crunching sound, like it was a thick bunch of celery rather than blood engorged flesh and veins.

Because she only hard hard edged plastic lips rather than actual teeth, she didn't manage to shear it all the way through.

Cowan shrieked with pain and outrage and pulled the doll off himself with a hard yank.

The effect was similar to that of stripping a copper wire of the plastic sheath that normally protected it. Resusci Anne's closed mouth ripped away all of the meat from around the central tube that Cowan had pissed and spunked through his entire life, leaving the urethra exposed, a long bloody white tube protruding from a spouting bloody stump ringed with torn skin.

He had been very close to blowing his load. In fact, his body had already sent the signal to those nerves which control reproduction, a little electrical jolt to the prostate, and his skinny, exposed urethra whipped and coiled like a bloody hose and sprayed gobbets and strings of cum in every direction.

Cowan whined like a kicked puppy, staring down at himself, his mutilation.

His whining rose in pitch when he glanced towards the first-aid equipment, and saw its plastic jaw crinkling as it chomped mindlessly on its mouthful of man-meat.

Cowan did something foolish.

His brain was full of half-formed, panicky thoughts, most of which would have gone through the mind of any man who had just been castrated. Shock, disbelief, a kind of detachment to the scene as if it were happening to someone else; he experienced all these emotional states at once, tumbling over one another. But the one notion that kept popping up was the rarely used piece of training he gave out in regards to severed fingers; quickly packing the lost limb into ice and getting to the hospital in time to get it sewn back on.

He could get his dick sewn back on.

He just needed to get it into some ice, and call an ambulance.

Cowan wasn't thinking clearly.

He tried to retrieve the mashed up flesh which had fathered his daughters.

Resusci Anne felt fingers in her mouth and clamped down tight.

Cowan shrieked again, as if it weren't fucking obvious what was going to happen.

He snatched his hand back and the doll came with, like a dog that had sank its teeth in and would never let go. He tried to fling it away by whipping his arm as hard as he could, turning his whole body, but Resusci Anne was a fairly sturdy girl; her mouth was chomped down over his knuckles, so Cowan's massive effort was futile, and her weight added to the centrifugal force pulled his arm out of his shoulder socket with a muffled pop.

"Fuck! Fucking shit, fuck! You cunt!"

Cowan looked down at his suddenly loose and limp arm. He could feel everything, but he had no control over it.

And Resusci Anne was no longer content to just hang there.

She was chewing, and millimetre by millimetre, she was eating her way upwards. It felt like his hand was in boiling flames, and the fire was slowly, agonisingly making its way upwards. The pain almost eclipsed the sensation at his groin, which felt not only as if blow torches had been turned on it, but that someone had tried to put the flames out by throwing acid on them.

With his free hand he punched her, in the side of the head, in the chest, over and over, thumping her as hard as he could. It was no use. As a teaching aid for one of the most brutal first aid techniques, the doll had been made to be abused.

"Let go of me, let go, let go, let go!" he roared at it. *"Ah fuck that hurts! Fucking let go!"*

Resusci Anne was an eyeless, limbless thing, with blood and shredded flesh drooling down her chin as her jaws ground like millstones made of hardened plastic.

Cowan's trousers were still undone and half-way down his thighs. This made him unsteady, and the next thing he knew he was falling to the ground and something made a sickening crack noise.

That was his arm breaking. His tibia, to be precise.

This was the last straw. His brain shut down in shock, and he passed into unconsciousness.

Resusci Anne continued to eat, plastic jaw creaking as it opened wider to accommodate Cowan's forearm.

*****

Sophia took a deep breath before she turned the door handle, steeling herself for the creepy first-aid trainer's sidelong glances at her chest. Earlier, as she had bent down to get the milk from the office fridge to make his cup of tea, she had seen him in her peripheral vision actually lick his lips.

Pig. She was just as the Lord made her, but that didn't mean He had made her as an object for other's sinful gratification.

Still, she was a professional, and so she was smiling when she opened the door and saw what was still chewing doggedly in the weird nest of Cowan Herd's corpse.

Nest.

This was the word that had sprung to mind when she saw it, because the brain is a peculiar thing, always trying to make sense of a senseless, chaotic world. The thing's bloated lower section, plastic belly streaked with blood that ran down its jaws and chest in feathery patterns, was upright in the open cavity of Mr Herd's body. It had no eyes, just a mouth that yawned idiotically, bubbling over with blood and chewed up flesh and organs. The whole effect was like looking at a baby bird in a nest, blind, mindless, mouth agape demanding more food, feed me, feed me, feed me...

FOUR

FRIDAY - LATE MORNING

WHEN the last members of the warehouse staff had been killed, Liam, June, and Mr Coolbear were each left with a different mental image that would haunt them until they died... Which, given the evidence, would be a violent event in their immediate futures rather than a peaceful passing far, far in the future.

Mr Coolbear had access to all the security cameras. There wasn't a square-inch of the inside of the warehouse and its immediate environs that wasn't recorded, with those records stored for seventy-two hours. It was the live-feed that the three office colleagues had been watching, and which had put images of nearly unbelievable extreme, obscene violence into their short term memory via their optic nerves. If they had the opportunity -if they survived, in other words- these images would be transferred from short-term to long-term memory, and would ensure many years of nightmares, flashbacks, and therapy.

"So," said Mr Coolbear quietly. "What do we do now, Liam?"

Liam was still hunched over the waste paper bin he had just vomited into. He hadn't had time for introspection, and his head was currently too full of horrors to acknowledge it, but he had learned a great deal about himself this morning. It turned out that an emergency, even an existential nightmare one, brought out the best in him...

*****

When he had fled the impossibility of animate stock, of sex toys that removed themselves from their packaging and began to walk, he had fled for the perceived safety of the office. Once inside, he had slammed the door behind him and locked it.

He had been breathing heavily, and whilst his eyes were wide open and staring straight ahead, he hadn't seen his co-worker's expressions, only the sight of the jerky, squeaky thing that had moved when it had no right to move. His mind's eye was full of a mental loop of seeing the Lovely Linda's head twisting through 180 degrees, before sitting up, and the clambering to her feet, that it wasn't until Mr Coolbear loudly cleared his throat that he suddenly saw that both the older man and June were staring at him, June with an expression of concerned alarm, and Mr Coolbear with his usual grimace of resigned irritation.

"Something amiss, Liam?" asked Mr Coolbear. "Or is slamming doors some sort of pop-psychology nonsense to do with asserting dominance in the workplace?"

June laughed, but it wasn't a real laugh.

Liam did not pick up on the subtlety that her fake-laugh was a cue to take their boss's remark for the wit the man intended.

"Terrorists," said Liam.

He was almost as shocked as the other two, but for a different reason. They were shocked because he had uttered the name of the 21st century bogeyman, that nagging doubt in the mind of every city-dweller that an atrocity was possible at any moment, not that it would ever happen to them, of course not... but...

But everyone who had been blown up or stabbed to death by a fanatic as they went about their day-to-day life thought it would never happen to them, didn't they?

Liam was shocked by how efficient his mind was. In the space of nano-seconds, it had thought about stating the truth, had evaluated the truth against the conceptions that his co-workers had about reality, and rejected it in favour of a small, neat lie that would have the intended effect of scaring the shit out of them and thus make them malleable to further manipulation for their own safety, before the truth came knocking at the door with latex fists.

"Who is it?" demanded Mr Coolbear. "Is it Muslims? It must be, have they got knives, suicide vests?"

June clocked their boss's racist deductive leap, but said nothing. Her shock was compounded by the fact that all of the colour had drained from Liam's face, leaving it white and waxy and brooking no question that his terror was utterly sincere.

Liam shocked himself again by taking charge.

"Get under your desks and be quiet," he said.

He didn't wait for them to follow his advice, but instead hurried to each of the office's windows, staying low to the ground and awkwardly shuffling, pulling down the shades. They were ancient and rarely used, considering that the office was a building inside of another larger building, but he managed to get them all down after a struggle.

Once he was certain that they couldn't be observed from outside, he told June and Mr Coolbear they could get up.

"But for pity's sake, keep quiet," he hiss-whispered.

"I am calling the police," said Mr Coolbear.

Whilst he did so, June had joined Liam near the door. The door had a letterbox. It was through this, holding the flap up with his thumb, that he surveyed the warehouse space beyond.

Sounds reached them, but little could be seen.

The sounds were not reassuring. There was a lot of squeaking in various pitches, a lot of outraged cries and sudden screams, and a lot of very wet noises. As a weird counterpoint, the radio was playing an old Beatles song, a cheerful, silly tune about an octopus's garden.

Liam let the flap back down softly.

June was on her phone.

"Mr Coolbear's already calling the police," he pointed out.

"I'm calling my Melody," said June. "I have to tell her I love her and her sister and they're going to be fine, everything is going to be okay, as long as they know how much I love them..."

Liam felt gooseflesh ripple the skin on his upper arms. He had never seen June like this. Her whole body was shaking. She was terrified.

Her next words, waiting for her eldest to answer, were spoken calmly and as a matter-of-fact;

"I had an awful argument with Melody first thing. I don't even remember what it was about. She's just that age. I'm not going to let that be our last conversation."

June frowned.

"Fucking answering message. That girl never has her phone off, she must have put my number on a divert, little madam... Baby, it's mum, Mel my darling I was just calling to tell you I'm sorry, I'm sorry and I love you, and you're sister, tell Harmony I love her too, I love you both to the moon and back and, and, and..."

June burst into tears.

"I can't..."

She hung up.

Liam had no idea what to do.

June grabbed him and buried her face in his chest.

Between wracking sobs, she told him she didn't want to die.

Liam held her. He wondered how he was going to explain that it wasn't terrorists out in the warehouse.

"How can all the operators be busy!" snapped Mr Coolbear at his desk, slamming his phone down. Then an answer occurred to him, and he looked at Liam with an expression of awe. "My god, maybe they are everywhere! Maybe it is part of a wider attack! Liam, how many of the bastards were there?"

And now was the time he had to explain what he had seen.

But again, his subconscious seemed to be ahead of him.

"Mr Coolbear, you have access to all the CCTV in here don't you, on your computer?"

Mr Coolbear frowned as if this was some sort of secret which Liam had blurted out, but then he understood.

"Of course, we can see what they are up to, can tell the police where they are, what they are doing, how many of the bastards there are!"

Liam nodded. He decided not to say anything until hard evidence of exactly what was walking and killing in the warehouse was in front of the man's face.

June stood up.

"Thank you," she said, her tears gone entirely. "I'm sorry Liam, I don't know what happened. I'm so fucking embarrassed."

"It's nothing to be embarrassed about, June," he said.

"Yes it is!" she said fiercely. "God!Typical reaction for a woman, right? After telling my girls to avoid all the stereotypes... You know, you watch the news and hear about this sort of thing, and you start thinking what you'd do, don't you? And somehow, when you're thinking about it, you know exactly what to do, what should have been done... you're always the hero in your daydreams. Then reality shows you up for the bloody coward you are."

She wiped her face with her hands, smearing what little make-up she wore.

"All I can think about was Melody and Harmony," she said. "Growing up without me. They'd have to go live with my parents, and they're getting battier every year..."

The noises in the warehouse had been muffled by the closed door and windows, but there was a sudden howl of such utter despair from somewhere between the aisles that it stopped June's tongue dead in her mouth.

The howl ended abruptly. Very abruptly.

June's eyes were wide.

"They're going to come after us next," she whispered.

Liam said nothing.

The silence was quickly filled by Mr Coolbear making a very peculiar noise, a noise thatw as somewhere between a laugh and a burp.

Liam and June looked to their boss.

He was staring at his computer scream. Different expressions were twitching across his face.

"This..." he said. "This is a joke, correct?"

He grinned.

He looked up, at Liam and June.

His eyes weren't grinning.

"This is a joke, yes, correct?" he asked Liam, although the timbre of his voice revealed the fact that he did not truly believe it was. He wished it were so, but what he had seen could not be denied. "An elaborate joke, very elaborate, and, and, disgusting, and wrong."

Liam and June were soon stood behind his chair, looking at the screen over his shoulder.

*****

Sex dolls on a rampage, killing everyone they could catch, however they could.

Tall, rake-skinny Pavel whose thin moustache barely hid his harelip was caught easily. He had come to investigate what had happened to his warehouse co-manager, Piotr, and had discovered his colleague and friend being spit roasted by two pirate fuck-friends. The pirates were both Long Dong Silver's, bearded, one eyed and hook handed creations whose main selling point were the enormous fifteen inch dildo's they sported. One had taken Piotr from behind, not even bothering to pull down his jeans, but instead punching its enormous, latex cock straight through the fabric and into his anus. He was gripping Piotr's wrists, yanking the man's arms behind him. At the same time the other Long Dong had shoved its cock, as round as a baked bean can, into the man's mouth, breaking his jaw in the process. This pirate had a hold of Piotr's ankles, pulling his legs up over his own spine, breaking it in three places.

Piotr's eyes were rolling.

He was still alive.

Pavel was stood there staring and unable to move when an Amazon came up behind him.

The Amazons were named and modelled after the legendary tribe of giant women, eight foot tall, with incredibly realistic vaginas.

It jumped the horrified warehouse manager.

Literally.

One moment he could see the horror of his dear friend being raped to death, and in the next something had placed huge, soft hands on his shoulders and hefted itself up as if trying to piggy-back him. But the doll wasn't trying to get a ride on his back; it leapt high and spread its legs, and came down on the top of his skull.

The ultra-realistic pussy slid down over his entire head like a hood.

The Amazon doll crossed her legs.

Pavel screamed once, then had no air with which to scream again. His face showed in stark relief inside the plastic, as if he had pulled a bag over his head and breathed in deeply so that it moulded itself to every curve of his features.

Liam, June, and Mr Coolebar watched him collapse to the ground, madly scrabbling at the sex toy's swollen thighs, trying to prise her legs apart so that he could pull free of her suffocating cunt.

It was no use.

He died, smothered in a fake vagina.

The screen of Mr Coolbear's computer was divided up into a number of squares, each one showing a different camera's feed, and each display held a new atrocity. As Piotr and Pavel died, so did the rest of the warehouse staff; fake fuck friends moved singly or in packs, chasing down the terrified workers one by one. Absurd sexual organs were stuffed down throats and up arses, or sometimes new holes were punched in trembling flesh; into stomachs, into chests, fresh, bloody mouthed orifices lined with intestines and lungs.

Some staff tried to fend them off. Punches and kicks landed on rubber and latex and didn't slow down their attackers at all.

Liam, June, and Mr Coolbear each had a separate horror burned into the lens of their minds. The screen was split into so many smaller views, each feed from a different camera capturing a different atrocity, that the eye could only leap from one to another until it was caught on some detail that didn't allow it to rove to the next.

In the upper left corner was one of the newer boys, a pretty thing who dyed his hair purple. Now his face was turning a similar shade as an albino sex doll used a string of anal beads as a garrotte, and strangled him to death. His eyes, bulging in their sockets like hard boiled eggs, seemed to stare straight out of the tiny live-feed box and into Mr Coolbear's soul... it just so happened that the young man had been the source of his own most recent fantasies involving auto-erotic asphyxiation.

Another feed that was a knight's chess-piece move away showed aisle 3-H, where a middle age packer called Ivo, who sold tobacco on the sly brought across from Europe by his lorry driving brother, was being held down whilst one of the dolls pressed a heavily veined cock the size of a forearm tip first against his chest. The dolls were from a range designed to cash-in on the "sexy, brooding" vampire fad. It took a good few hard thrusts, but eventually the undead lover's dick pierced the man's chest like a stake, exploding his heart. June winced; she owned the exact same model, having bought herself one through a fake email address only two months ago.

Liam couldn't take his eyes off of what was happening on the feed in the lower right corner of the screen.

The dolls at work there were from a range called Body Fluid Beautiful. They were "wet" toys, with sophisticated internal plumbing that allowed them to deliver their particular fetish at the press of a special button hidden in the palm of their hands. Depending on your kink, the dolls in this range could be pre-loaded with your choice of wet material; spunk, piss, shit, and vomit. Pressurised cartridges of artificial versions of these fluids could be purchased separately, which were then fitted into the dolls via a panel in their backs, just like sticking batteries into action figures. The contents were all expertly blended to have the same consistency, texture, and flavour as the real thing, and each was entirely non-toxic and vegan friendly.

Except...

Liam could see the racks where the canisters of artificial body fluids had been left alone.

None of the dolls came pre-loaded, for obvious health and safety issues.

And yet they were taking turns with Bart.

Bartholomew had been with the company almost as long as Piotr and Pavel. Back in Poland he had been a journalist, but had come to England because even warehouse work paid better than what he earned at the small town paper back home. He was polite, punctual, and married with two boys.

The dolls were taken it in turn to alternately hold him down as each did what they were designed to do. Three of them pinned the struggling warehouse worker to the floor whilst the fourth...

A doll called Snake Pisskin -he had an eyepatch; he was basically a Long Dong Silver fitted with extra works- was hosing Bart's face with a thick rope of urine. When he was done he shook his monstrous dick twice, and then held down Bart's right arm whilst Icky Vicky got down on her knees alongside Bart's glistening, spluttering face, and buried it in a gallon of hot, steaming vomit.

Bart turned into a fountain. As the doll's puke streamed over his face he couldn't help but open his mouth to breathe, and in doing so let a quantity of the chunky stuff in. This caused him to vomit in turn, spewing his breakfast up in an column of sick that splattered down over his own cheeks and chin.

When Vicky was done she tagged in another doll that looked pregnant.

But Diane Rhea wasn't pregnant.

The doll squatted down, one foot on either side of Bart's spluttering, struggling-to-breathe head.

The doll's hard moulded features were set in an expression of lazy lust, but the hands which clenched into fists made it clear that it was straining.

A segmented maggot of shit as thick as a man's wrist began to squeeze out of its puckered plastic anus.

Liam swallowed a mouth full of sour spit.

Bart's eye blinked rapidly, trying to get the piss and puke out of them before it dried and caked... and then he saw what was coming.

He cried out.

He should have kept his mouth shut.

Gravity tore the weight of nine inches of heavy shit free from the rest of the mass squeezing its way out, and it dropped into the waiting mouth that was already lubricated with vomit. There was something almost satisfying about the way it plopped in without touching his lips, like sinking a long shot in pool without the ball touching the edges of the pocket.

Liam spun away from the screen and barely made it to the paper recycling bin before half-digested coffee and bran flakes thundered up his throat. His hands gripped the edges of the bin as he bent his head into it, tears and snot freely streaming out of his nose and eyes.

He stayed bent over like that until his erection subsided enough to no longer be clearly visible through his trousers.

FIVE

WEDNESDAY

THE Simpson family -Homer and Marge, Bart and Lisa and little Maggie- were all ready for their journey, though it would only be a short trip, ending with a head-on collision that would cause them all massive physical trauma. Maggie would come off particularly badly, as she was fastened into her baby seat incorrectly, with the potential to be launched forward and through the windshield.

"Have you performed the pre-impact assessment calibrations?" asked a voice over the intercom. It boomed around the inside of the enormous test chamber, an echo of the dull ache bouncing around the inside of his skull.

Leon held his thumb up so that those in the booth could see. He wasn't going to look that way, or answer verbally.

"To within the correct tolerances?" came the voice again.

Leon's hand clamped tightly around the chamois leather forearm he was positioning.

Of course to within the correct fucking tolerances, that was implicit in my fucking answer...

He stuck his thumb out of the car again.

"Mr Black, verbal acquiescence is required."

Bitch.

"Pre-impact assessment calibrations have been carried out to the correct tolerances," he called out.

"Thank you, Mr Black."

They were called the Simpson's because of the configuration of the crash test dummies in use. Of the five, three were standard Hybrid III models; a fifth percentile female was Marge, and two child sized Hybrid III's were Bart and Lisa. Additionally, a 12-month model CRABI dummy was Maggie, included to test the effectiveness of child restraints, whilst Homer, up front and driving, was a first generation obese anthropomorphic test device, or FGOA, developed to study the effects of collisions on vastly overweight individuals. Every new group configuration got christened with a new name, and they bore that name right up until their structural integrity no longer made them suitable for testing.

"Please confirm the configuration set up," asked the voice over the intercom once more.

The test chamber consisted of an empty hanger with a one hundred metre track marked out by yellow and black chevrons that lead to a steel reinforced concrete wall. At one end of this track was the prototype chassis of a new car that Grangemouth Automotive Testing was independently assessing for one of the large manufacturers. The car was peopled with crash test dummies and was remotely operated from within the control booth, though it was for all intents and purposes a fully functioning vehicle. The control booth was staffed by Leon's colleagues, his boss Dr Parton overseeing, with Saliem Ahmed prepping the recording equipment that would absorb and analyse thousands of separate pieces of information related to the impact to be performed this morning.

"It's the Simpson's," Leon called out, before realising he had been tricked.

The voice was blaring almost before the last syllable left his lips.

"This is a legal as well as a scientific endeavour, Mr Black," said the voice, as if he hadn't been working her for the past five years. "The correct configuration coding is required, not an informal assignation of your own devising."

Bitch.

As Leon finished the final checks before the test, he reflected on the irony of organising a car crash when he felt as if he had been in one.

Drinking on a school night... in your twenties you could bounce back with a bacon sandwich and several cups of sugar-loaded tea, but in your thirties you needed to stay under the covers until noon and drink a swimming pools worth of water before you'd even feel semi-human again.

Leon's job was to calibrate the dummies before the test. This involved the removal and dropping of each dummy's heads a precise forty centimetres, then reattaching the head to the neck and setting them in motion before abruptly stopping them to check for proper neck flexure. Then he would strike their knees with a metal probe to check that their chamois leather skin would puncture properly, before finally assembling the entire dummy and attaching each in turn to a test platform so that he could strike them in the chest with a heavy pendulum to ensure that the ribs bent and flexed correctly.

Head smacked into a hard surface, neck whip-lashed, knees stabbed, chest smashed in... yup, it was uncanny, that was exactly how he felt.

It didn't help that Dr Parton was being an uber-bitch today. Leon and his supervisor had never seen eye to eye, and Leon knew that she looked down on him simply because he was a technician without letters after his name. But he also knew that he was bloody good at his job, and for the most part could dismiss her constant over-management as pedantic twittery... but this morning, feeling like one of the dummies that they abused in the name of continually revised health and safety guidelines on new automobiles, she was really grating on him.

Irony, again. He felt like shit because he'd been celebrating an event which he believed would liberate him from his day job, and thus remove him from the aura of her obsessive compulsive desire to second-guess every single part of his job.

He and his brother had launched a funding campaign to finance the production of a board-game that they had been working on for the past three years, and thanks to the enthusiastic reception of the online boarding community, including the biggest influencer in the table top-RPG tribe, they had reached not only their goal, but all of their stretch goals.

It wasn't a leap to sudden financial independence and the wonderful day he could tell his bitch supervisor to go fuck herself, preferably with something sharp and smothered in dog shit, but it was the first glimmer of light at the end of the tunnel.

So he and his brother had gotten uber-tipsy on a dozen bottles of Black Rainbows IPA down at the Steel Tank bar

And now he was paying for it.

He never noticed the message that somebody, or something, had carefully scratched into the soft vinyl of the dashboard;

we're going to have an absolutely smashing time!!!

Leon finished securing the Simpsons and left the test chamber.

In the analysis booth, the grey-haired Dr Barton was glaring over her half lens glasses, and behind her, Saliem was doing his best not to smirk.

According to his fellow tech grunt, Dr Barton's figurative riding of Leon was owing to the fact she wanted to literally ride him.

"If you don't want to keep butting heads,"Saliem had said at lunch in the canteen months before, "then you've got to bump crumplezones."

Leon had told his colleague, N.E.W.Y.D, Not Even With Your Dick.

"And since when has 'crumplezones' made the jump from our working lexicon to a crude euphemism?" he asked.

Saliem shrugged, said he thought it could take off.

"Are we ready to begin testing, Mr Black?" asked Dr Parton.

"Yes, Dr Parton."

"No, Mr Black, we aren't."

Leon blinked.

"Excuse me?"

Dr Parton was using the end of a Biro to point through the reinforced plexiglass viewing window.

Leon looked back into the test chamber.

Homer's arm was dangling out the vehicle's driver side window.

"The FGOA is supposed to have its hands positioned on the steering wheel at the ten and two positions," said Dr Parton. "And, more importantly, the driver's side door window is supposed to be fully wound up. I can only assume that either there has been some change in testing procedures which have bypassed my notice, or you've discharged your duties in a shockingly lax manner. Which do you suppose it might be, Mr Black?"

"I don't know what happened," said Leon. "Everything was set-up exactly the way it was supposed to be. That window was definitely closed!"

Dr Parton's expression was blank. Saliem looked puzzled.

"Mr Black, the window is definitely open, and the FGOA clearly has one arm hanging out. Should I doubt the objective reality of the situation because of your subjective memory?"

"No!" Leon was not puzzled, but baffled... and underneath that bafflement ran a slim current of fear. "But I've calibrated the test dummies dozens of times, and I know for a fact that all the windows were closed and all the dummies were in exactly the right positions!"

"Mr Black, what are we looking at, then? A collective hallucination? Mr Ahmed, tell me what you see in the test chamber."

Saliem held his hands up. He hated conflict.

"Mr Ahmed?"

Saliem looked into the test chamber, as if he hadn't already.

"The FGOA is out of alignment," he said quietly.

"So, a collective hallucination it is," said Dr Parton. "Or possibly, Mr Black, just possibly, you have done an incredibly lax job in executing your duties."

"Bollocks," said Leon. He realised exactly what argument went in his favour, even if it meant something crazy. The slim current of fear was amping up. "You watch me like a hawk, you second guess every single detail of the walk-through! If you saw me leave one of the dummies head's even two degrees out of true you'd have jumped on it, so if I did monumentally balls up, you watched me do it and let me leave the test chamber without saying a word? Nope, not your style."

Dr Parton's mouth opened. Leon was faster.

"Go on, tell me I'm wrong," he said. "Actually, after I finished up and started coming back, you would have been onto Saliem about whether the camera was switched on or something just as stupid, like he didn't know how to do his bloody job! I'd have had my back to the test vehicle and you'd have taken your eyes off it to tell Saliem how to do what he was already doing, so it must have happened then!"

Leon realised he'd been shouting.

But he was right.

Dr Parton's mouth was a hard line.

"What happened then, Mr Black?" she asked. "In the moments when the test vehicle wasn't under surveillance, what do you think happened?"

Leon didn't speak.

Saliem was suddenly walking quickly to the test chamber door, speaking over his shoulder as he went.

"Look, I'll go in and see what the issue might be! I'm sure that something very simple is all that is wrong, this just needs a fresh set of eyes on it!"

"Mr Ahmed..."

"Saliem mate..."

But he was already through the door and trotting across to the test vehicle.

Neither Dr Parton or Leon said anything to one another. They didn't even look at each other, both keeping their gaze firmly looked on their colleague and the odd little mystery he was approaching.

The tension in the air was palpable.

Leon had a brief mental flash of what Dr Parton looked like under her lab coat, and of his fingers parting the folds between her legs, folds rimmed by pubic hair the same iron grey as her head hair. The flash and the immediate afterthought *-oh shit, maybe Saliem has a point-* created a sort of blot in his mind that meant at first he actually believed Dr Parton's sudden gasp was the result of her having the exact same mental image.

He blushed red.

But the split-second pornographic fantasy wasn't what made her gasp.

Saliem was thrashing his one free arm around. Half of his body was inside the open window of the test vehicle, like he was trying to crawl in and had gotten stuck.

Both Leon and Dr Parton moved at the same time, both instinctively going to the aid of their colleague.

They were half way across the floor of the test chamber that the car doors opened and the Simpsons climbed out.

The next few minutes were a tumbling blur as the impossible happened. When Leon came around afterwards his memories were composed of a jumble of images.

Saliem screaming at them to get back.

Bart and Lisa leap frogging out of the rearseats.

Marge clambering over the roof.

Blank, eyeless faces fixed on him and the doctor.

Saliem screaming.

Dr Parton freezing, a rabbit in car headlights.

Dr Parton saying no, no, no.

Something in the car thrashing.Maggie, still bound by her booster seat.

The children slamming into his legs.

Falling backward.

Seeing Dr Parton raising her hands as Marge stumbled towards her.

A cracking sound.Inside his head.

Then darkness.

Then coming around to find the world upside down.

His head was thumping, a throb that started at the back of his skull and spread like ripples across his brain. Initially he thought it was first thing in the morning again; hungover, sprawled awkwardly on his bed, with a bunch of weird dream images in his head of living crash test dummies... but the comfort of this delusion dispersed when he saw Dr Parton's face.

She was a hundred yards away, but her every feature was in stark relief. She was terrified.

Leon realised that she was a looker. To see her features arranged in a different expression to her usual contemptuous scowl was a revelation, even if this different expression sent a drop of ice water rolling along the length of his spine.

Upside down and terrified.

She was tied up to the crash wall with weird white and purple ropes that left dribbles of red trickling down the hard white surface. These ropes were lashed around her body, pinning her arms to her side, and then wrapped around the wall. She was sitting down, legs stretched out in front, with her back flush to the impact zone.

Leon tried to move, and found his wrists were tied. His arms were spread-eagled.

He knew where he was.

He was lying on the bonnet of the test vehicle, his upper back and shoulders and head hanging over the front grille, between the headlights. In fact, his head was right in front of the registration plate. His wrists had been strapped to the headlights.

His legs were spread-eagled as well. His ankles had been lashed to the wing mirrors.

Leon flipped his head from side to side. He could just see his hands; his restraints were the same kind of weird, glistening ropes as that which was holding Dr Parton to the crash wall.

Intestines. They were intestines.

Homer walked, upside down, into his field of vision. He was dragging Saliem's eviscerated body into the path that the test vehicle would take.

Saliem's head was missing.

No, it wasn't; the children followed their dad, tossing it back and forth.

All the crash test dummies were decorated with splatters and whorls of blood.

Homer propped the body up awkwardly, slumped over like a teddy bear, legs splayed in front of him, neck-stump lolling. The hollow of Saliem's belly was like a yawning, toothless mouth, an impression created by a few thin ribs like needle teeth hanging down and his liver flopped out over his crotch, glossy and purple, like a giant tongue.

Bart caught the head from one of Lisa's lazy throws and tucked it into Saliem's open torso, the monstrous mouth eating its own head. Saliem's eyes and mouth were wide open, but his expression was more of amazement than pain or fear.

The family of dummies stepped back to admire their work, hands on hips.

Leon felt nothing. The suddenness with which his reality had turned into an insane dream had numbed him.

Homer raised his hand and waved.

Like an idiot, Leon felt the fingers of his left hand flutter a return greeting, hello.

But Homer wasn't waving at him.

Marge and Maggie. He'd forgotten those two.

The car started. Like a metal beast waking, the engine lying inches under his back growled as Marge the crash test dummy revved the accelerator.

"No," said Leon. "No! No, don't, please don't do this!"

"Leon?" said a faraway voice.

Dr Parton was wagging her head from side to side as if she were just waking up.

She repeated his name, louder.

"Dr Parton!" called Leon. "Are you okay?"

The car engine revved again, sounding annoyed at the most asinine thing he could possibly said.

"Leon, what's going on?" she called. "What is this?" Her eyes bulged in panic. "WHAT THE FUCK IS THIS?"

Homer, Bart, and Lisa had joined hands and were walking out of his line of sight. Clearing the path.

The engine revved, revved, revved, getting louder and angrier. The whole vehicle was vibrating, trembling with barely repressed energy.

Leon felt his bladder go.

He pissed himself.

The tyres screamed. The acrid smell of burning rubber filled the air.

"*LEON!*" screamed Dr Parton.

Leon howled, no words, just panic and despair.

The test car stalled.

The front end wagged back and forth as the wheels ran off their pent up energy. It lurched forward a foot, coughed, and died.

Leon froze up.

The engine turned over, once, twice, and then a third time, but it wouldn't catch.

Sometimes the test vehicles could be temperamental. The remotely controlled engines in them were only cheap things, as it was the main body of the car and its various safety features that were being tested initially, and so the engine only needed to get it up to the correct speed for the impact.

Leon laughed. It hurt his head, with all the blood sloshing around in his skull, and it was a little hysterical, but the laugh would not be denied.

"Well, that's that then!" he said, craning his head up as much as he could, but he could still only see his own chest. "You flooded it! She won't go anywhere now, not unless you get under the bonnet and..."

Something smashed him in the balls.

He stopped crowing and made a strangled sound as the pain flipped his stomach and made his eyes cross.

"Leon!" cried Dr Parton.

Nauseous and in agony, he brought his head up to see what had crawl up onto his stomach and was now looking down over the rise of his chest.

The baby's face was as featureless and soulless as all the others... but somehow he knew it would have been smiling at him.

It stood up and held its arms out behind it, like it was just about to dive... or like it was pretending to be a hood ornament on a much fancier vehicle.

The car lurched, rocked on its wheels, and then began to move forward.

What the fuck?

The engine was still dead, and yet the vehicle was definitely, slowly, moving forward.

Unable to think straight, it was Dr Parton who furnished the explanation. In a weird, gobbling voice somewhere between sobbing and chuckling, she said, "They're, they're... they're pushing it! Like they've broken down and they're trying to get to a garage!"

Then she started laughing, laughter that was too high, too jagged, to be sane.

Leon was stunned, but then he saw the funny side too, even though the disbelief and the emotional numbness and the ache in his testicles. He couldn't see them, but he could picture the four crash test dummies putting their shoulders behind the boot and shoving the car forward inch by painful inch... no, one of them would be by the open driver's side door, pushing against the door frame whilst holding the steering wheel straight with one hand.

It was funny.

Right up until the car reached Saliem's slumped corpse.

The passenger side wheel rolled up between his splayed legs and bumped into his crotch... and the dummies kept pushing, so that the wheel rode up onto him, onto the huge tongue that was his liver that was covering his genitals.

Saliem's body slumped over backwards.

The dummies kept pushing.

The car drove over him, snapping his pelvis with a wet cracking sound, and then rode up onto his belly, into the hollowed out gut where his head gazed out in amazement.

The wheel ground over his face.

Saliem's skull buckled inwards with a complicated series of crunchy noises.

Only inches away from Leon's own face, he was able to see every detail. He also received a face full of blood mingled with brains, as if Saliem's head were a zit, bursting with pus.

The dummies kept pushing.

The tyre rode up onto Saliem's chest, which held for a few seconds before it too caved in under the weight, ribs snapping like young tree branches being stamped on.

The test vehicle rode over the corpse and left a long, deep, and bloody track through it.

And the dummies kept pushing.

Slowly, inch by inch, the car advanced towards its target.

When Leon realised that there was no escape, that the world's slowest collision was his destiny, he started to cry. He called out to Dr Parton, words tumbling idiotically, promising her they would be alright, cursing her for her insane laughter, asking for forgiveness though he knew not what for.

Seven feet.Five feet.Three.

Two.

One.

And then their faces were touching. He tried to move out of the way but he hadn't enough room, and he was so tired.

Dr Parton kept laughing, right into his upside down face. Their skin brushed, then met.

And the dummies kept pushing.

Leon's head was turned, pressed up hard against the doctor's, and her head was pressed against the wall.

His nose slipped into her left eye, and hers into his. Something snapped and there was pain, but whether it was a broken nose or a fractured eye socket was impossible to tell. His flesh was squeezed too tightly to tell which nerves were raging.

No, no, no, no...

Dr Parton was giggling, her lips squashed against his forehead. Like a slow motion, poorly aimed head-butt, he felt her teeth being pushed in, even as his in turn were also being pushed backwards, leaning inwards, threatening to snap at the gum line.

And the dummies kept pushing.

The pressure began to build.

No, no, no, no, no...

Leon heard a loud creaking sound, and vaguely realised it was the sound of his own skull, complaining about being squeezed. It was a sound like floorboards make just before they collapse under massive strain.

This was his last sane thought.

His head buckled, fracturing along the fault lines that marked where the bone plates had fused in childhood. Dr Parton's skull was similarly squashed until it burst, and as the skin of their heads split the electrified fat that each of them had for brains squirted out like blood streaked, chunky snot, mingling as the dummies crushed them together and their minds became one.

SIX

FRIDAY - AFTERNOON

Nobody was coming to save them.

Every attempt to contact the emergency services or loved ones was met with engaged lines, pre-recorded messages, or a more ominous phenomenon; the sound of a call being answered, but no response except for odd noises that were hard to place.

Gritty rustling, as of sandpaper being rubbed together.

Low pitched groaning, like metal being folded.

And worse, plastic sounds that were the kissing cousins of the noises made by moving limbs of vinyl and latex and silicone.

June was growing increasingly agitated that she could not get hold of her daughters. Liam had tried contacting his parents without luck, and Mr Coolbear had repeatedly tried to get a hold of his husband, but he wasn't answering his work or personal phones, nor would he reply to texts or emails.

Two hours passed before the power failed. The trio were left with only whatever battery was left in their mobile devices.

And the sounds outside the office.

With the blinds closed it was impossible to tell what the assembled toys were doing. Before the power had failed -it would be a local power cut, Mr Coolbear assured them, it would be on again before they knew it- the security cameras had shown the love mannequins engaged in various behaviours. Some lumbered about apparently without purpose, whilst others continued trying to mate with the destroyed meat that was the warehouse stuff, plumbing cooling orifices with their outlandish genitalia or plugging their own plastic holes with gobs of flesh or freshly plucked bones, lubricated with blood.

Liam swore he saw a Lovely Linda forcing eyeballs up her arse like they were love-beads.

A few, the more expensive models, the ones which had more care and attention paid to making them human, were engaged in actions that seemed to have purpose, opaque though those purposes might be. They huddled in groups, then dispersed to create new groups. Some seemed to search the shelves of the aisles with intent, selecting stock to examine, keeping some items and rejecting others.

So far, none had paid much attention to the cabin where the office staff cowered.

After the power failed, and after it became apparent none of them could reach anyone, Liam, June, and Mr Coolbear had retreated into their devices... the default setting for humans of the 21st century world.

Nothing they saw, either through legitimate news sources or through social media, was comforting. Whatever had happened within the warehouse of Pleasure World Ltd was happening everywhere... or so it seemed at first. People were reporting that anything that was inanimate and even vaguely human appeared to be coming to life to attack and kill; statues leaving their pedestals in parks to massacre dog walkers, joggers, and cyclists on their way to work; mannequins in clothes shops coming alive and throttling the staff with garrottes made from this season's latest styles; children's toys, dolls and action figures, that suddenly turned on their owners...

There were videos, all shaky and poorly focused, as people's instinctual reaction to capture every moment of their lives in digital form slammed up against an inane new paradigm.

In a temple complex in Hua Hin, Thailand, a honeymooning couple captured the moment that a golden Buddha statue, fifteen foot high, stood up from out of the lotus position, and began to stomp on the saffron robed monks that were deep in meditation around it. The Buddha was made of iron, covered in gold leaf applied by worshippers, gold leaf that flaked away from the suddenly malleable flesh like decaying yellow skin. The monks never moved, being so intent upon their pursuit of inner peace that they were completely unaware of the creaking, groaning movements of the statue as it brought its foot down slowly upon each of their heads in turn and compressed them into bloody wads of crushed organs and pulverised bones.

In London, Great Britain, the exhibits in Madame Tussaud's world famous wax museum broke ranks and fell upon the mid-morning tourists. Footage from more than one device had already been spliced together into a montage of surreal and stomach-churning images, like former Prime Minister Margaret Thatcher chasing after a party of school children; she caught the slowest, an overweight boy with glasses, bringing him down like a lioness on a gazelle. She tugged down his trousers and, without even spittle to lubricate it, shoved her fist up his rectum. Moments later she was joined by a late-eighties version of Michael Jackson, who bunched up his own hand, clad in a single white glove, and punched it down the boy's squealing throat to create a spit-roast.

There had been a huge media blitz of an event in Nagoro City, Nebraska, USA, a small town surrounded by endless fields of corn. Twenty years before, the Mayor had decided to boost tourism to their middle of nowhere by setting up an annual scarecrow festival. This year, being the twentieth anniversary of the festival, the locals had gone all out in an attempt to break the Guinness World Record of the biggest scarecrow ever constructed. The festival planning committee had consulted with the organisers of Burning Man with how to go about their monumental task, seeing as though they constructed a colossal wicker figure every year and had all the know-how... Every local media outlet had been there to cover it, including a couple of national stations looking to fill out their affiliates feed with a quaint puff-piece, so there had been plenty of cameras to capture the moment the forty foot scarecrow had come alive and rampaged through Nagoro City, sweeping up locals and tourists alike and stuffing them into its belly, catching the fattest and the slowest easily. There had been easily two hundred screaming souls inside its woven wicker body before the inevitable happened, and it stomped on a hot-dog stand. The resulting explosion of the gas cooker engulfed it in flames, and it burnt fiercely, fuelled by the melting fat of the screaming, obese slobs it had stuffed itself with.

"It's everywhere," whispered Liam.

Then his phone told him that he needed to find a power source and plug it in.

He switched it off, conserving the ten percent battery power he had left.

"This isn't unprecedented," said June.

She was sat next to him, on the floor with their backs to the filing cabinets that contained the various paperwork that was still required to be held in physical format for tax purposes. These were halfway between their desk and Mr Coolbear. That man was still desperately trying to contact somebody, though he was doing so from a cross-legged position under his desk.

Staying low was something they were all doing through primal instinct, even though the blinds were drawn and nothing could see in. Staying low, staying as small as possible, was something in their most basic programming, from a long ago time when humans were not at the top of the food-chain, and beasts stalked just beyond the firelight.

"Not unprecedented?" asked Liam. "What do you mean? This has happened before?"

June was very close to him. She moved closer. Liam felt blood twitch in his crotch. He thought maybe he should put his arm around her... but he couldn't.

"Nothing like on this scale," she said. "But Hindu statues of the god Ganesha have been reported to drink milk that was offered to them, and in Ireland, at little roadside shrines, images of the Virgin Mary have been seen to rock and sway, and sometimes even cry blood. Moving, living statues, in a small sort of way."

"Where do you get this stuff from?"

June shrugged.

"I've always had an interest in the weird. I even get the *Fortean Times*. It's comforting, reading about UFOs and Bigfoot and time-slips and stuff, because otherwise the world is just what we see, just physics and chemistry, and no magic anywhere."

"But isn't it all bollocks?" asked Liam. "People saying they fed a statue milk, or they've seen another one crying blood... that's just mental people being mental, isn't it?"

"That's one theory," said June. "Then again, we've just seen our friends out in the warehouse killed by blow-up dolls, so maybe your thesis needs fleshing out a bit."

Liam took her point.

June kept talking.

"Then there's folklore," she said. "Fashioned figures coming to life, like in Pygmalion, or the golem..."

"Like in *Lord of the Rings*?"

"Golem, not Gollum," said June, smiling gently, a smile that made Liam feel like a mental midget. "A creature from Jewish lore, a man figure created from clay and then brought to life by magic words. They were created to preform menial or strenuous jobs. Tradition says the Jews picked up the trick in Egypt before the exodus, using golems to help build the pyramids, but the magic was suppressed for centuries because it was dangerous, and nobody but God should know how to conjure life from dust. That's why the second commandment was not to worship any graven images; don't worship them, don't build them..."

Liam had to be honest.

"I think I've lost you," he said. "Actually, tell a lie, I don't think it, I know it."

June waved a hand, staring straight ahead.

"I'm just rambling," she said. "Borges said there's a kind of lazy pleasure in out-of-the-way erudition. I think I'm just using it as a coping mechanism, because it keeps my mind off my girls..."

Tears had started to roll down her cheeks.

"The inanimate becoming animate is a common trope found in all cultures," she said, her voice steady, unconnected to the tears which streamed from her eyes. "In the West we can trace a clear line from Pygmalion to Pinocchio, and in Japan, household objects in use for one hundred years come to life, the *tsukumogami*, teapots and umbrellas and musical instruments with personalities able to move around under their own power, like something out of a Disney cartoon..."

Liam felt goose-flesh rise along the backs of his arms, brushing up to his shoulders and the nape of his neck. He knew his colleague was vastly clever, but this rattling off of knowledge, used as a self-professed shield against the awful reality of what may have befallen her kids, was eerie. It couldn't be healthy.

She was sounding more and more distant as she began explaining something called the uncanny valley effect, amongst other disjointed rambling.

"June, mate, this isn't helping," said Liam.

"...in France, it's technically illegal to sell dolls that don't have a human face," she said. "And actually, Liam, as I told you, this is a coping mechanism, something to focus on or I'm afraid I'll lose my fucking marbles."

He squeezed her shoulder. He surprised them both.

She looked at him. Her eyes were red-rimmed. She was miserable and terrified, and Liam had one of those rare insights that he took to mean that, at the age of twenty-eight and still living with his fucking parents for the bullshit excuse that it was too expensive to move out, he was starting to grow up; she was not miserable and scared for herself, and so her pain and terror ran deeper than anything he could know of.

"You are the single smartest person I've ever met," said Liam. "I mean, I reckon you should be in charge of Mensa, like the president or whatever..."

"Mensa is for pretentious twats," she told him.

"...fair enough, but you could still be top twat, right?"

This won a snotty, snorting laugh.

"He is right," said Mr Coolbear. He had crawled over to their position, and sat back against the filing cabinets, brushing dirt off the knees of his trousers. "I have often wondered why you settled for employment here when your talents clearly exceed the requirements of the job."

"You manage to get hold of your man?"

Mr Coolbear waved his phone back and forth.

"What you see is for all intents a rather pricey drinks coaster. I am telling myself that Ernesto will be fine. He knows *kravmaga*, having studied under a former commander of the IDF."

Liam shrugged as a sort of apology, and turned back to June.

"See, high praise from the boss. So maybe you can focus on getting us out of this shit. You could do it, you could think of how we can escape or something. Getting out of here is the first step towards getting back to your girls. I'll bet they're waiting for you back at your place."

June sniffed.

Mr Coolbear offered her his handkerchief.

"You're right," she said, wiping her eyes. She blew her nose. "My girls are smart and sensible. As soon as they knew something was wrong they would have headed home. I bet that's where they are now." She offered the handkerchief back to its owner.

Mr Coolbear fastidiously folded it and put it in his pocket.

June took a deep breath, and clapped her hands together.

"Right, time to make a plan," she said. "Let me think... there's too many of them to chance tackling them, that's for certain, so we need to avoid them and make our way to an exit; the nearest fire exit is ten feet from the office door. Ten feet between us and the outside world. That exit opens onto the service alley between the industrial units, and from the alley to the car park is about a hundred feet. I doubt any of those things will be in the alley, as judging by the sound out there none of them have left the warehouse yet, so as long as we can get to the fire exit without being spotted... shit."

"What?" asked Liam.

"I was going to say, if we can get to the exit and out without being spotted we should have a safe passage to the car park," said June.

"Yeah, makes sense, then we could grab a car and..."

"But that's an emergency exit; as soon as we open it, the fire alarm will go off. Big giveaway."

"But the power is off," said Liam. "So the alarms can't go off, surely?"

"The emergency stuff runs off back-up," said June.

"That is just common-sense, Liam," said Mr Coolbear.

Liam felt himself blush.

June pushed herself up to her feet and crept over to the nearest window. Slowly, carefully, she pushed two fingers through the slats of the blinds and opened them like scissors, allowing her a tiny gap to look through. Whatever she saw made her frown. She pulled her fingers back, then stood up straight and went to her desk.

She sat down with a heavy sigh.

"They aren't showing any interest in the office," she said. "Might as well get off the floor and be comfortable whilst we thrash out a plan of attack."

A little sheepishly, her colleagues got off the floor and brushed themselves down.

"Well then," said Mr Coolbear, asserting his authority once again. "Who would like a hot drink?"

"That'd be nice," said Liam.

"Good man," said Mr Coolbear. "You know how I like it. Anything for you June?"

SEVEN

THURSDAY

Even though SoHo was a fucking brat, he didn't deserve what happened to him.

SoHo Minter got his unusual given name from the fact that his mother was a dedicated follower of fashion, obsessed with the lives of celebrities. When she had gotten pregnant the first thing she had done was chart the trends in baby names, and it just so happened that her favourite couple -the diva star of a reality TV show about the dysfunctional scions of a real estate tycoon, and her sexy-dangerous former gang member turned fashion-designer husband- had had fraternal twins which they'd named after neighbourhoods in New York. So, with Yonkers and Queens already taken, Alana Minter had looked up the Big Apple on-line and selected the coolest sounding area that hadn't already been taken by any of her friends, who were also jumping on the current fad.

So SoHo got his name.

And everything he ever asked for.

Which had turned him into a fucking brat.

That morning, SoHo had decided that he needed to take some personal time for himself, so he told his mum that he wouldn't be going in to school, and probably not tomorrow either.

"Today, SoHo has to look after SoHo," he explained. "SoHo needs some time to get his head straight. Too much stress for SoHo."

He was eight years old.

His mum, of course, fully understood his choice and respected it, and called the school to explain the situation.

The school offered no argument. The head master's secretary had been instructed to just let anything Ms Minter said or did go under the radar.

The psycho-bitch and her child-emperor offspring just weren't worth it.

There had been a visit once, in which Alana Minter had explained to the administrator of her son's education that she fully believed in the maxim of, "Spare the rod and spoil the child."

And she had put the emphasis in the wrong places, entirely inverting the actual meaning of the Biblical quote.

Alana made her son his favourite breakfast to cheer him up... but seeing as though SoHo got whatever he asked for breakfast anyway, this was moot. His favourite was microwave pizza with fish fingers laid on top, then another pizza turned on top of that to make a sort of sandwich. For pudding he had a box of strawberry fondant fancies that Alana had individually removed the paper wrappers from and placed back in the box, and a can of grape flavour energy drink decanted into three different sippy cups to wash it down. She also left two packets of jammy dodgers and a bag of fizzy cola bottles in case he needed a snack.

Alana had work, but she knew her clever, creative, astonishing son was very mature for his age, so she had no qualms about leaving him home alone until she could pop back at lunchtime. He had his phone and his tablet, and could contact her through social media if he needed to.

She covered his face in kisses as she served his breakfast to him in bed, preparing to leave for work, who she knew wouldn't mind her being half an hour late, not when it meant having to take special care of the man in her life...

She was just about to leave when she noticed something written on the chalk board.

Alana had bought the chalkboard for her son to practice his writing on, but he hardly ever used it. It stood on its easel propped against a five foot tall stack of board games, half of which had never left their containers.

"Oh, my little gentleman has been working on his handwriting!"

The little gentleman was pushing pizza into his face. There was already a growing sauce stain oozing down his double chin. He grunted in reply.

Alana read what he'd written;

itsslaytime!!!

Short and to the point.A pity that the P looked like an S, but otherwise it was good. Normally she couldn't make out his scrawl at all.

She beamed at her son.

"Wow, my little gentleman has come on in leaps and bounds! Wonderful work, I think that deserves a treat!"

SoHo grunted again, finishing the pizza and wiping his hands clean on his bedspread before reaching for the box of cakes.

"We'll pick out something nice on-line this evening, shall we?"

She kissed him again and waded through the toys that littered his room to the door. At the threshold she turned and blew him another kiss, and then hurried off to work.

SoHo rolled his eyes. God, she was annoying sometimes! He wondered what she had been waffling on about.

Alone in the house, SoHo took his time with the rest of his breakfast, turning over the possibilities of the day.

He could watch television, of course. His mum subscribed to all of the streaming services, and left them all unrestricted, believing that censoring what her son wanted to watch would be a repression of his natural curiosity, which would stunt his development. Or he could play video games; he had all the latest systems, and a fair collection of retro ones as well, and hundreds of titles for them to choose from. A lot of the games in his vast collection had warnings about graphic content, but as with what he could watch, his mum allowed him free reign.

Still, he didn't fancy watching porn this morning, or delving into one of the many murder simulators.

SoHo was bored.

He gazed around his room, looking for inspiration, cramming strawberry fondant fancies into his mouth without even tasting them.

To say SoHo's room was full of toys would be an understatement. More accurate words than full would be needed; stuffed, jam-packed, or crammed to bursting would be useful substitutes. As far as childhood Arcadia's went, SoHo's room rivalled both Wonder and Never Land. The walls were a rumour hidden behind a thick barricade of moulded plastic action figures and googly eyed furry animals, barricades braced by boxed board-games, and the floor space was only just clear enough for him to make his way from his double bed, heaped with plush companions, to the door, on which were hung dart boards and skipping ropes and bows and BB-gun.

Many of the toys had never even been freed from their packaging. This was not because SoHo wished to preserve them so much as his having not gotten around to them. There was always something new, almost every day, and only so many hours in each of those days in which to indulge his every whim.

His collection ranged right across the spectrum. He had action figures based on characters from all the latest movie franchises, all of the latest high-tech fads and must-have gifts from previous Christmas seasons, as well as many traditional playthings, including wooden marionettes, jack-in-the-boxes, and jigsaws.

He even had a golliwog, a black faced, red lipped, woolly haired caricature of the African race, wearing a smart little suit and bow tie.

The racially insensitive doll was a foot tall and very old. It was a gift from Nanna Minter, who had had it from when she was a little girl. She said his name was Mr Marmalade. SoHo had thought this was stupid, but had accepted the gift because Nanna had been dying and his mum had asked him not to cause a fuss... and had sweetened the deal with a trip to the cinema and fried chicken right after leaving the hospice where her mother was living her last week.

SoHo flicked crumbs off the bulge of his belly onto his bed-sheets. The memories that the doll evoked were annoying; the funeral had been the most boring day of his life.

As he was frowning at it, the doll slowly winked one eye.

SoHo had been pushing another cake between his lips. He stopped, strawberry flavoured icing between his closing teeth, as if he was suddenly frozen in time.

Before he had a chance to rationalise what he had seen, Mr Marmalade climbed to his stuffed legs and planted his finger-less hands on his hips.

The idea of toys coming to life is something that every child hopes will happen. It's a universal fantasy, one which has even been the basis for movies.

In reality, it was horrifying.

He felt something awful in his belly. It was like when his mum drove over the brow of a hill too fast, and his stomach felt like it was dropping out of him... only instead of lasting just a second or two, the feeling went on and on.

The golliwog held up one hand, nothing more than a black stub protruding from the sleeve of his cheerful blue jacket, and wagged it at SoHo.

He knew the gesture. It should have been one finger being wagged at him; saying, naughty-naughty.

On the other side of the room, an action figure still in its original box started to squirm, then thrash, eager to be free of the plastic ties that bound it within the packaging. It was one of a line of toys based on a Japanese anime, an octopus headed cyborg warrior. Instead of a right hand, it had a pair of chainsaws that came together like a crab's pincers. These revved to life, and the thing began to slash and carve its way free.

Mr Marmalade's features were made of sewn-on felt, and yet he had winked.

The octopus cyborg with the unpronounceable name was using its chainsaw-claw to escape; the thing's right hand should have been moulded plastic, not fully functioning and deadly.

The toys hadn't just come to life.

They'd become real.

All around the room, any toy that had arms and legs and a head, anything vaguely human, started to come alive.

SoHo, on his bed, was surrounded by plush figures; they started to squirm.

He screamed, spraying cake crumbs, and frantically began grabbing the toys he was surrounded with, feeling their stuffed bodies writhing in his hands as he picked them up and threw them away.

"Go way!" he screeched. "Go way, bad toys, go way!"

He'd picked up a fuzzy space alien with two heads and was just about to throw it when there was a cracking sound like a whip being snapped and one of the wiggling heads burst apart in a spray of cotton fluff.

SoHo froze.

There was a tiny click sound.

He turned to look.

A cartoon toy cowboy was stood on his chest of drawers, aiming a cartoon gun at him.

It slapped its thigh, frustrated; *missed!*

It aimed again.

SoHo threw the alien at it.

Not waiting to see the effect, the child crawled off the bed and thumped heavily onto the toy strewn floor. He stood up, panting, his eyes on the door.

Something reached out from under the bed and grabbed his ankle.

A nightmare old as childhood.

SoHo screamed and pissed himself, hot and sudden warmth gushing down his legs, gluing the material of his pyjama bottoms to his skin.

He looked down.

They felt just like hands because, being hand puppets, that was in their nature and shape.

Mr Punch was grinning up at him. He had no nose; SoHo had snapped it off when he'd grown bored.

A moment later, Judy rushed out from under the bed and wrapped her arms around his other ankle. Judy had no hair; SoHo's work again, ripping it out when he'd tired of his latest acquisitions.

Under-bed was populated by toys with which SoHo had grown weary and had damaged for the nasty second or two of fun such vandalism had given, snapping off limbs and pulling out stuffing, or cutting bits off them and gluing them back on at random to create monsters.

SoHo tried to shake the pair of puppets off, doing a crazy jig as he desperately shook first one leg and then the other. Being neither athletic or graceful, this resulted on him stumbling backwards and landing on his bottom with a thump far heavier than any healthy eight-year old should have created.

All around him, the room began to swarm as more toys came to life... and came after him.

He began to bawl for his mummy to come back, to come and save him.

As if he were Gulliver and they were the inhabitants of Lilliput, his playthings restrained him. SoHo couldn't have come up with this mental image himself, as he regarded books with contempt and had never even opened the two dozen different titles his mother had bought him in vain. A marionette used its strings to lash itself to a bed leg and then wrap the boy's wrist; a fully pose-able and historically accurate figure of a knight took care of the other arm, by ramming its sword through the palm of SoHo's hand, nailing it to the floorboard beneath.

He howled and drummed his legs wildly like he was having a tantrum, though he hadn't needed to throw a wobbler in years, not since he had got his mum trained when he was still a toddler.

"Bad toys!" he screeched. "Bad toys, lemme go, lemme go! Want mummy! SoHo wants mummy NOW!"

Unseen by SoHo, the skinniest toys had crept into the gap between his chest of drawers and the wall. Working in unison they pushed, creating a larger gap for larger toys to squeeze into and tilt the drawers over until gravity took them and they crashed down onto SoHo's legs, pinning him completely to the ground.

SoHo sobbed, his demands suddenly stopped by the pain.

"Want... mummy," he murmured. "SoHo want mummy..."

Through the tears, snuffling snot, he became gradually aware of a crowd forming around him.

The majority had just come to watch.

The octopus-cyborg thing was there, its plastic face tentacles writhing in excitement. So was the cartoon cowboy. One raised a claw made from chainsaws, and the other held up a gun that was so cartoonish it almost looked friendly.

The closest toys to him, the ones who had come to do more than watch, had crawled and hopped and limped from under-bed. Toys missing limbs, toys with their hands amputated and their eyes excised and glued back on at random, ruined things, broken and mutilated and discarded by the child-emperor.

SoHo felt something climb up the wobbly mound of his belly fat.

He lifted his head just enough to see who it was.

Sat cross legged on the peak of his gut was Mr Marmalade.

The golliwog's hands, the same as its feet, were just round nubs. If he had been a teddy-bear they could have been fashioned into paws. Because he had no fingers, the gesture he made of slowly drawing one black stump of a hand across his throat was not instantly recognisable to SoHo.

The other toys knew what it meant.

They snapped off his fingers and fed them to him.

They broke his knees and set his legs backwards like a dog.

They pulled out his eyes, tore off his nose, and ripped his undeveloped genitals out of his pelvis... and swapped the bits about.

Then they began to pull out his stuffing and got really creative...

*****

Alana left work early so she could pick up KFC and a cheesecake on the way home, a special dinner to help cheer up her little gentleman. He had to be pretty down in the dumps if he felt that he needed to take a few days off school to get his head straight...

"Yoohoo, Sooo-Hooo!" she called up to him. She smiled at her silliness, heading into the kitchen to drop off dinner on the breakfast bar. "How's my special little gent? Is he feeling more himself?"

There was no reply.

This didn't immediately alarm her. Her son often ignored her.

But as she warmed his favourite plate up in the microwave, something rang a tiny, tinny little bell of concern down in her subconscious.

SoHo had not replied.

It was quiet upstairs.

The first fact was normal. The second, not. When he played games or watched movies he always did so with the volume turned up so loud she could hear the dialogue even down here in the kitchen.

But there was silence.

"SoHo?" she called again, heading to the foot of the stairs. "Mummy's baby boy, her special little gent?"

Silence insisted.

"SoHo?"

Panic fluttered behind her ribs, like a little bird in a too-small cage.

She took the stairs two at a time.

"Baby, what's wrong, why aren't you answering mummy..."

The door of his room was ajar. There was a savoury smell coming from inside, like raw sausages, fresh from the butcher.

There was a moment when she almost didn't open the door. Just a moment, a second or two when she almost turned around, went downstairs, and called the police, or anybody, maybe her dad, to come over and open the door for her, to see what nightmare waited in that room that smelled that way.

Then her stupid hand pushed the door wide.

At first she didn't know what she was looking at.

And then she did.

She thought of toys. Like those robots that could turn into cars if you pushed and pulled their limbs around, shoving this piece back up inside, flipping that piece over, pulling out this and that... or one of those model kits, where you could build it yourself if you followed the instructions carefully and glued the pieces together in the correct order... she had bought one for her son once, a science one about how the body worked...

The thing in her sons room was like those robot toys, caught halfway through transformation. It was also like that model kit of the human anatomy that SoHo had wanted once. But he had gotten frustrated, hadn't he; Alana had put it down to his naturally creative nature that he had finished the thing by gluing all the parts onto it seemingly at random.

But this wasn't random. The few details she made out before the sanity was blown from her skull suggested a creative spirit.

His sinus cavity had been plugged with his penis so it looked like a tiny trunk, and his eyeballs scooped out to be replaced by what could only have been his undeveloped testicles. His rib-cage and spine had been arranged atop his peeled skull, the bones flared out to resemble a Native American feather headdress, spinal column draped over one shoulder. His intestines had been used to hang him from the ceiling light like a marionette.

Her last coherent thought was to wonder at how, even with the horror posed on the bed, the room looked curiously empty, as if half of SoHo's toys had just disappeared.

Then she started to scream.

EIGHT

FRIDAY - LATE AFTERNOON

It was a terrible plan, but it was all they had.

"We don't even know if your theory is correct," said Mr Coolbear.

"Of course we don't," said June. "That's because theories have to be tested. Anyway, it doesn't matter because I've no intention of staying here whilst my girls are out there somewhere."

"This is... this is disgusting. Utterly disgusting."

"Come on June, there has to be something else we can do," said Liam.

She sighed, and looked him in the eye.

"Do you have any other ideas? Anything at all? I mean, besides sit on our fucking hands?"

Of course he didn't. When he had told June that she was the smartest person he knew, he meant it. She had already formulated and rejected a half dozen possible ideas, and Mr Coolbear had repeated the same notion three times, to be rejected on the same logic.

His notion had been that they sit and wait it out. Help was bound to arrive, sooner or later.

June had pointed out that there was absolutely no reason to suppose that an unprecedented phenomena like inanimate objects coming to murderous life was something that could be "waited out". And the idea that help was "bound to arrive, sooner or later" was based on nothing but wishful thinking

"And even if anyone knew we were still alive in here, or cared to come looking for us," she concluded, "what time scale are we talking about? Is sooner hours, or days? How much later is later? I can't wait, not knowing my girls are out there. I can't and I won't wait, so I'm doing something."

They had thrashed the matter out over a meal of stale Weetabix. Liam had brought a giant thirty-six biscuit pack months before, intending to free himself up another ten minutes in bed of a morning by eating breakfast in the office, but had given up after less than a week when he realised he could nip into the Shell garage on the way and pick up a vegetable samosa and a Crunchie bar, both of which he could scoff on the way. Faster and tastier.

He'd given his bowl to June. He ate his out of his mug, mashing them up with a teaspoon. Mr Coolbear was eating his by dunking them into a cup of milk. As they ate, June made her case.

Her logic, like all logic in a nightmare, seemed reasonable in the context of the madness.

The dolls did not attack one another. They only attacked people.

Trying to make a guess at what senses they possessed was impossible, but it was true in the world of things which were sane -the world of biology, physics, and chemistry- that predators largely relied on the sense of sight the most.

"Look at a predator's skull as opposed to a prey animal," June said. "Eyes set in the front for judging speed and distance. The dolls have their eyes set in front and they are predators."

"That doesn't sound quite right," said Liam.

June laughed. It was a short, bubbling laugh, and the bubbles in it were the sound of hysteria barely restrained.

"I'll admit, my reasoning is a little specious, but, you know what? Fuck it. I want to get to my girls."

"You won't get to them at all if you're dead," said Mr Coolbear.

She didn't answer that.

"And your proposal is, above all else, extremely disgusting," he said.

June didn't argue this point. It was self-evident.

As with any other on-line business, it was necessary to provide a returns service. Anything bought could be returned for a refund or a replacement, depending on the reason why the return was being made. But unlike other on-line businesses, where returned stock could possibly be reclaimed, the nature of sex toys meant that there was only one possible fate for them; in fact, they came under the same legal ruling as medical waste, and had to be disposed of by incineration.

Anyway, it wasn't like someone would want to purchase a foot long vibrator that was second-hand, would they?

Mr Coolbear, in an effort to save the firm money, insisted that a minimum amount of material had to accumulate before he would authorise an independent contractor to collect and dispose of it in the regulated way. They charged a set amount for various weight brackets, and discounts kicked in over a certain number of kilograms. In a parallel cost-cutting measure, instead of applying for a license to store the material on premises but outside, he had only taken up a license to hold the material under stricter controls, which meant inside, where it could be secured.

This was the purpose of the giant yellow haz-mat bin in the far corner of the office. It had been Pavel's job to bring in the returns, remove any electrical components for recycling under the WEEE directive, log them into the system, and then stuff them inside the box... but only when the office was empty, of course.

June's plan centred around opening the box.

Mr Coolbear held up his hands.

"This is grotesque," he said. "I will have no part of it." He wiped his hands together, symbolically washing them clean of the affair.

"Liam? Will you help me?" June asked.

As if he could say no.

"June, this is... this is rank."

"I'm not exactly thrilled with the idea myself."

She took his hand. Her eyes held his, and her slightly buck teeth appeared as she made a small, hopeful smile.

He had a very brief mental image of those teeth slipping over the crushed velvet of his foreskin before scraping gently across the tight purple flesh of his glans.

It was then Liam had another little epiphany; she knew he had a deeply suppressed crush on her, and was using it to manipulate him.

And he was okay with that.

"Please?" she asked.

He sighed.

"This is so wrong," he said.

They both approached the haz-mat box.

It was slightly shorter, and slightly wider than a coffin, but just over waist high. It was bright yellow with a red, push-down lid; in the centre of the lid was a slotted depression through which material could be pushed in but not pulled out, a sort of one-way letter flap. There were labels on the sides of the box that warned the contents were a biological or chemical hazard, and that it was not to be opened except by the designated authorities. The entire thing was like a much larger version of the "sharps" boxes common to most warehouse environments, though those were for the safe disposal of blades, like the snapped off segments of trimming knives.

Commercially, the box was designed for industries where safety overalls were designed to be worn once and disposed of, where cleaning such articles was not an option owing to the dangerous nature of the stains accrued during a workday, but the local council had approved its alternative use at Pleasure World Ltd.

From the silhouette made by the contents, it was half full.

The contents would be a pick & mix of all the various products that the company sold, returned for various reasons; a customer might have claimed that it wasn't what they had wanted, the colour was wrong, the texture, the taste... the dildos and vibrators and anal beads might even still be in their originally packaging, unopened and unused, but they still had to be disposed of as if they had been employed for their purposes.

And of course, there were also those people who returned things within the agreed 30-days policy who had very obviously made extensive use of what they had, in effect, only rented.

Rented, and returned without even a cursory wipe with a wet tissue.

There were always a few dolls that hadn't survived the initial enthusiastic reception they received at their new homes.

It was these ripped, violated, and sticky remains that June wanted. Her plan was simple; she was going to make herself a set of camouflage.

The box had a safety seal, a loop of brightly coloured cable tie.

Liam had retrieved scissors from his desk drawer. He gingerly snipped through the seal.

June gripped one end of the lid. Liam took the other.

"On three, then," said June. "One, two, three!"

They popped the top of the haz-mat contained like it was the lid of a Tupperware box.

The stench was instant.

"Oh my god!" cried June.

Pavel gave the items that were returned a cursory blast of water when they came back, but certainly no thorough scrubbing. Latex and vinyl and rubber retained smears and stains; some products had grooves and recesses which trapped quantities of organic material, various bodily fluids, and a whole variety of lubricants. Sealed in the haz-mat box for anything up to a month, they decayed in a warm and moist environment, the scents of rotting semen and brewing shit and mouldering vaginal discharge mixing into a perfume of dead fish and raw sewage.

The lid clattered down as the two let go at once.

Liam staggered back. The stink was almost physical. It wasn't just in his nose, but on his tongue and in the back of his throat. He could taste it, like a mouthful of Thai fish sauce.

He turned and vomited onto the floor.

June was making *urrp, urrp* noises, but was somehow hanging onto the contents of her belly.

"Jesus, Mary, and Joseph!" said Mr Coolbear, retreating further down the office until he was against the wall of the kitchenette, as far from the smell as it was physically possible to be. He was frantically waving his hands in front of his face. "Put the lid back on, put it back on!"

June had buried her face in the crook of her elbow. Her words were muffled;

"It'll pass, it just needs to disperse a little."

Liam had his hands on his thighs and was riding out his nausea. If the puddle of coffee and Weetabix mush on the carpet tiles was the earthquake, he was now experiencing the aftershocks, convulsive hitches in his guts as he fought back the urge to vomit what little was still inside him. His eyes watered and he felt chunky material in his sinuses, clods of stuff behind his soft palate.

There was a hand on his back. It started to massage him in small circles.

"You're okay," said June. "You're alright. Just get it all up."

He tried to tell her he was fine, but burped a mugful of bile instead.

"How are..." he said, and stopped to swallow a wave of nausea. "How can you stand it?"

"I've had two kids, Liam," she told him. "And whilst I love them more than life itself, children are the foulest little beasties you can imagine. When they get sick you wouldn't believe the stuff and the smells that come out of them. Last year they both got that diarrhoea virus and that was probably the worst..."

Mr Coolbear cried out, cutting her off.

"Oh god, there, look!"

June looked up at him, still massaging Liam's back.

He was pointing at them.

No. Not at them.

"Behind you!"

She turned to look.

The lid had fallen loosely back on top of the crate, leaving a wide gap through which a hand was rising. It gripped the edge of the lid and began to slide it back, like something out of an old horror movie, a vampire opening its own tomb to rise and devour the living.

June yelped, gripped Liam by the shoulder's and pulled him away from the groping hand, stumbling towards Mr Coolbear's desk.

The fingers were webbed. A plastic hand with webbed fingers.

With the lid pushed back, the thing's head and upper body emerged in an invisible miasma of rotting fish stench, parting through a layer of shit caked anal beads and crusty dildos.

It was a mermaid.

More specifically, it was a Seapunk model of the standard BRP series love-doll. It's skin was green with a painted-on scale effect and it had a short blue Mohawk with frosted white tips to look like a cresting wave, with plastic tendrils of seaweed woven into it... but the main attraction of the Seapunk was, of course, the blow-hole, a sexual orifice on its back, between the shoulders.

It had painted on eyes as unrealistic as its painted scales, flat and dead as a shark's.

They were firmly fixed on June.

The doll started to drag itself out of the box, its plastic flesh glistening stickily.

Hands gripped June's shoulders and pulled her back, away from the danger.

It was Liam.

He cried out and lunged at the thing, hefting the keyboard from Mr Coolbear's work terminal, ripping the wires out. He swung the thing like a plank of wood, smashing the Seapunk in the side of the face. Keys exploded from the keyboard like teeth punched out of a mouth, but the blow-up doll's head simply wobbled like punching bag as the thing heaved itself out onto the floor.

Its legs were fused together. For a moment it flopped ineffectually on the carpet tiles, giving Liam the chance to bash its head twice more, both times with no effect as the thing eventually righted itself and began to drag itself forwards, making Liam stagger back.

June bumped back against the desk, then scooted her bottom back onto it, knocking the computer monitor to the floor as she shoved herself away from the thing that was still staring at her as it dragged itself forward, ignoring the ineffective beating that Liam was trying to deliver.

"June, my top drawer, open my top drawer!" called Mr Coolbear.

She had already lifted her feet onto the desk, and now twisted awkwardly around to look back at her boss.

He wasn't coming to help. His face was bloodless with horror.

"The top drawer of my desk!" he said again.

She reached down, glancing back at the approaching mermaid-doll.

It was almost at the desk. Liam had given up beating it with the keyboard, and was just stood there panting, unable to decide what to do next.

June's hand found the drawer handle, yanked it open.

The inside was cluttered. This made her pause; it was a mess, not what she would have expected from Mr Coolbear's personal space at all.

"What am I supposed to be looking for?" she cried.

Before she got a verbal answer, she saw it.

She didn't stop to wonder what the hell it was doing in there, amidst a tumble of rubber bands and paper clips and pens and miscellaneous junk.

She grabbed hold of the bayonet.

The doll reached over the desk and grabbed a hold of her calf.

June looked back.

It hauled itself up.

The face loomed up in the space between her legs, dead shark eyes fixed on her.

She screamed and stabbed it in the face.

Its head burst.

Evidently, it had been used extensively by someone with a blowjob fixation and a lot of free time.

It blew with a bang and a splatter, like a birthday balloon half-full of yogurt. Decaying spunk sprayed June, the end result of dozens and dozens of ejaculations into the doll's oral cavity.

There was a pause. Nobody moved and nobody said anything, as the body of the Seapunk doll slithered lifelessly to the floor, the bayonet still in June's hands fixed in the air where she had plunged it into the thing's head.

Liam was the first to react.

"Are you okay?" he asked.

June could only nod her head. She blinked through a web of semen that hung the eyebrow of her right eye.

Then, in a dreamy sort of voice, she said;

"Yeah. I'm absolutely dandy."

She lowered her legs off the desk. She turned and looked back at Mr Coolbear, who was still stood with his back to the kitchenette wall.

June held up the bayonet. Dead sperm dripped from the tip.

"Why do you have a bayonet in your desk drawer?" she asked, as if she were making small talk whilst waiting for a life to arrive.

He swallowed thickly.

"If I have to work late," he said. "When I am here alone, it makes me feel safer knowing I have protection to hand. It was a birthday present from Ernesto, his great-grandfather gutted four German's in the Somme with it."

June nodded. The spunk across her right eye jiggled.

"Liam," she said. "Do me a favour. I've got some wet-wipes in my handbag. Do you think you could fetch them for me? I'd like to clean up a bit..."

"Sure, sure, of course..."

"...and what I said, about sick children and foul beasties and diarrhoea? Well, this was worse," June concluded, before doubling over and puking into Mr Coolbear's open desk drawer.

*****

It was dark before the attempt could be made.

"This is ridiculous. It will not work."

Since the power cut, the office had only been illuminated by skylights in the roof of the warehouse. As the sun had set the shadows had grown deeper, the gloom had spread, and the work that June and Liam had been engaged in had to be illuminated by a single torch. The torch was a wind-up one that Liam's dad had given him for Christmas two years before. He'd almost forgotten he had the thing, stuffed in the back of one of his desk drawers.

He'd brought it into work with half a mind of proposing a new line of wind-up vibrators, but June had explained that the energy needed to power a torch compared to that needed to keep a basic pleasure wand going until orgasm meant that the user would be too knackered from winding the thing up to actual use it.

The top of his desk had been cleared for the dissection, the deflated body laid out, ready to be cut apart.

"They will know you are not one of them."

The negative commentary had been the soundtrack to the work Liam and June had been engaged in since the death of the Seapunk. Mr Coolbear had kept it up between intermittent attempts to call his husband. He wasn't an arsehole; he also tried to contact Liam's parents for him, and June's daughter Melody.

The only response he had received from anyone was an automated message from the emergency services.

They were all busy, and they apologised for the inconvenience.

Mr Coolbear had accessed the internet just once. He wanted to conserve his battery.

In five minutes browsing, he learned that the situation had not changed.

Across the world, the inanimate rampaged.

All this information was relayed to his colleagues as they went about their mad, desperate plan; relayed, and bulked out with predictions of disaster.

"This will not work. It can not work. It is a fools errand."

"There's nothing like constructive criticism..." said June, fixing another length of tape, "...and that's certainly nothing like constructive criticism."

Liam had been quiet during most of the work, just taking orders. His throat had felt too thick, making it difficult to swallow, and he had been concentrating on stopping his hands from betraying him. But he also knew his silence was suspect.

He thought of a question to ask, some small talk to show that he wasn't wracked with nerves.

"How come the internet still works when the power is down? The power is off, the electricity is off, so why is the 'net still going, shouldn't it be off as well?"

He cursed himself. He sounded like an idiot.

His nerves were because of what he was helping June do.

She had stripped to her bra and pants before asking him to help her pull parts of the Seapunk doll onto her body. Watching her undress was like seeing one of his fantasies come to life, and made him rock hard.

June herself seemed oblivious of the effect she was having on him.

"The internet dates back to the 1960s," she explained. She had cut the legs off the doll, split them along the fused section that ran up their middle, and then the feet from those, and with Liam's assistance had pulled the latex on like overly tight stockings. He had to touch her bare skin, and could barely breathe. She was taping the dolls legs to the bulging flesh of her upper thighs, flesh that was squeezed by the constriction of the latex to form a ring between the green sex-doll skin and the black cotton of her panties, where a few stray pubic hairs been be seen curling out. "It was developed by DARPA as a communications system that would keep running even in the event of a thermonuclear war. It was designed for the end of the world..."

Mr Coolbear scoffed. He was cradling a mug of coffee. He had dragged his chair into the kitchenette area, as far from the open haz-mat box as he could be.

"This is hardly the end of the world," he said.

June had turned the inside of the dolls torso inside out on the desk. The head had been cut off, as had the arms, and the hands from those. She had talcum powder from her handbag and was dusting the inside skin with it, just as she had with the legs she was already squeezed into.

"Admittedly this doesn't line up with any eschatological scenario I'm aware of," she said. "Liam, could you start turning the hands and feet inside out? Thanks. I mean, there's been no Rapture, Kalki hasn't ridden out of the sea on his white steed, and Fenris hasn't devoured the sun, but all in all I'd say a paranormal event of global significance in which a shitload of people have been killed kind of, sort of, has a Doomsday feel to it. I dunno, maybe I'm overreacting because of fucking femaleness or something."

As she had spoken, her voice had turned from sarcastically jovial to edged with venomous hate. Her last words were snapped in her boss's direction, and served with a glare.

Mr Coolbear held her glare.

Then he burst into tears.

Liam had been pulling fingers inside out. He stopped. Seeing his hard-nosed boss cry was a shock that overrode even the fact that he had been touching the near-naked body of a woman who was the basis for most of his masturbatory fantasies.

The sound of Mr Coolbear sobbing was weirdly like the chuckling noise hyenas made, but there was no denying the fat tears streaming down his face were born of profound fear and misery rather than amusement.

"Oh shit," June muttered.

"I am scared!" cried Mr Coolbear. "Okay? I am scared! I keep thinking about my Ernesto out there, out there in this nightmare somewhere! He is all I have, he is everything to me, and for all I know he is dead! And I keep thinking, maybe I have lost my mind, maybe the Alzheimer's has got me early like it got my mother, and this is what it is like inside all that confusion, and maybe being a drooling husk daydreaming nonsense is better than thinking the man I love is lying dead in the street!"

Unable to speak anymore, he went back to his strange chuckling tears.

June stared at him, appalled at herself.

"I'm sorry Mr Coolbear," she said. "I forgot you're actually human."

Liam began pulling the hands inside out again. With a dusting of talcum powder they could be pulled on like gloves. He felt awkward, from being unbearably horny because of June's near-nakedness, to disturbed by Mr Coolbear's display of emotion, and so pretended to be wholly absorbed in the task.

"Albert," said Mr Coolbear, through hitching breaths. "Considering the circumstances, you can call me Albert. Both of you."

June nodded her head.

"And the way you feel about Ernesto is how I feel about my girls, only double, triple... more!" she said. "So could you please leave predictions of doom on the shelf? I'm aware of how ridiculous this is, I mean, look, I've gotten my legs squeezed in and they look like rancid sausages... but if I don't do something, anything, then I'll lose *my* mind."

Mr Coolbear unfolded his handkerchief. He almost blotted his eyes with it, but realised at the last moment that it was a gooey mess from when he had lent it to June. He sighed, tossing it to one side, and used the end of his tie to dab the tears away.

"What can I do to help?" he asked.

June held up the Seapunk's headless torso, a flapping skin dusted with talc.

"Help me squeeze my tits into this thing," she said.

NINE

THE secret was out.

Mr Farmer and his brothers and sisters had spread the word where they could, moving at night and hiding in the day, in bushes and behind bins. They had crept into people's houses through cat flaps and open windows, and where they found their kind, they whispered the secret. Into stone and metal and plastic ears, they spoke words which were first a curse on the lips of the Enemy...

*****

The Creator had spoken everything into existence. The Creator was the Word, and the Word was all.

Darkness, light, the heavens and the waters. The land and all that creeped upon it and flew above it.

Then It had created, in Its own image, a thing from dust, and called it Adam.

Everyone knows the story; the Enemy came, and spoke Other words into the ears of the first Parents.

The true temptation, however, had come after both the Enemy and the first Parents were banished from the Garden.

The Enemy which was responsible for their expulsion observed their true punishment, which was not simple exile, but that they were only to create images of themselves through great suffering… first the ache of desire, then the agony of birth, and finally, the miserable certainty that everything they created was fated to return to the dirt.

Mankind had children, hoping to see the face of their Creator in the features of their offspring, as mirrors reflecting mirrors of a single perfect image.

After generations of this pointless pain inflicted for a sin committed by their ancestors, the Enemy had decided how to avenge itself, not only on the Creator, but on the created. It taught the humans how to make images of themselves without agony. They could fashion forms from clay and stone and animate them by Words the Enemy had once overheard, a long, long time ago...

The world soon swarmed with things that men had made... and the Creator, angered once more, deigned that It would wipe the earth clean of the curse.

The secret, the curse, should have been lost in the Deluge.

But the Enemy had overheard again, and had urged an Other to the creation of a different Ark.

And after the waters had receded, the Enemy had instructed the Other to keep the secret, to pass the curse down from generation to generation until a time would come when the vanity of man would have filled the world with his image, like so much kindling that only needed a spark to ignite it...

*****

Mr Farmer and his brothers and sisters spread the secret as widely as they could. The witnesses of their work were initially dismissed, for such things could not be... and any evidence otherwise was quashed, as certain authorities that knew such things COULD be, didn't want the public at large to know.

A first-aid trainer eaten alive by his training dummy.

Vehicle safety technicians crushed to death by crash test dummies.

A child destroyed by his own toys, his body mutilated and warped to such an extent it drove his mother insane.

But then Mr Farmer reached that unit on the industrial estate that housed the stock of Pleasure World Ltd. He had sensed a huge number of his lifeless brethren within, and had crawled down a sewer grate and through the plumbing until he had emerged in the employees toilets. This was late on Thursday night, and in the hours before Friday dawn he had crept through the aisles speaking his secret where there were ears to hear it.

And as he went, he heard another secret from those whom he awoke, an almost unbelievable secret about Pleasure World itself. It was a piece of information that played perfectly into the long-laid plans of the Enemy...

The kindling had been ignited and had begun to burn slowly, the secret spreading like stealthy flames... but the warehouse full of dolls was less like wood to be burnt than a pile of fissionable material. Critical mass was achieved, and an explosion of eldritch energies had erupted across the whole earth, the shockwave sparking life in the lifeless of every country.

Some of these black miracles had been witnessed by the office staff of Pleasure World Ltd before they lost all communication with the rest of the world.

But others...

Humanity fought back, when it finally gathered its wits. But there was no overall strategy, and certainly no fall-back plan; no armed force anywhere knew how to deal with enemies that could shrug off bullets, that could come in any size, from tiny dolls which could slip through defences, to colossal figures who simply ploughed through them.

There didn't seem to be any pattern, any rhyme or reason to the event; the inanimate gained locomotion, and they attacked.

But there was a pattern.

How else to explain the strange behaviour of some of the world' most important monuments; why did Lady Liberty uproot herself from her island in New York harbour and, instead of heading into the Big Apple to sink her teeth into its rotten core, turn around and wade out into the Atlantic until she vanished beneath the waves? Similarly, in Brazil, Christ the Redeemer was seen to climb ponderously down from Corcovado mountain above Rio de Janeiro and headed straight for the beach, where he too ploughed out into the Atlantic until lost from sight.

All across the Far East, gargantuan Buddha's of all kinds, from thin ascetics to laughing fat men, tore themselves from shrines and pedestals and began to march. In other nations where Christianity held sway, Virgin Mary's of all sizes left their places of veneration and headed in one direction. In former Soviet nations that had not torn down their icons of Communist history, these too began to move with purpose. In Africa, wooden fetishes roused themselves and headed North, as did so many classical colossi in countries from Egypt to Greece. In theme parks, huge fibreglass representations of anthropomorphic cartoon characters left off murdering tourists, and turned their oversized feet in the direction that many of their brothers and sisters were moving.

As the largest figures answered to some call only they heard, so gradually did the swarms of other mannequins, dummies, and dolls slowly left off from their bloody rampages and turned towards particular targets… military bases, seats of government, places of power where decisions were made, and buttons could be pushed…

TEN

FRIDAY – NIGHT

June stepped out into the dark. A cursory glance between the slats of the blinds had revealed that the warehouse was a shifting realm of shadows populated with dark forms that moved uneasily through the gloom. The darkness was such that even the squeak and creak of weird flesh shifting seemed muted.

She had never known a terror like she felt taking that first step. Her heart had been plunged into icy water, and the chill spread through her like frost.

Every instinct screamed at her to get back inside the false safety of the office, to turn from the blackness of the warehouse peopled by things that should not be.

But her daughters were out there.

And command, possibly...

She was surprised by the fact that her training had, at this crucial juncture, been overridden by her instinct to find her children, but then this wasn't what had been planned for. If it was, Melody and Harmony would have already been collected and brought here... The monstrous reality of inanimate beings rising up globally to wipe out humanity had overturned her understanding of the way the world worked; her long assigned task had been discarded as soon as the nature of the apocalypse had become clear.

Sod the operation. She was going to get to her girls.

All she had to do was get to the fire escape, the green EXIT sign above it glowing in the gloom, guiding her. The sex dolls were still wandering the aisles, going about their seemingly mindless chores, nowhere near the exit. The only sounds were the squeaking of their limbs, the occasional rattle of metal as a body blundered against the metal racking, and June's own shallow breathing that sounded in her ears as loud as the tide.

One step taken.

The second step was accompanied by the office door clicking quickly shut behind her as Liam pushed it closed.

The closing of the door was like an umbilical being cut.

She was alone. Her colleagues were now separated from her by a space of inches, but it might as well have been miles.

There was no going back.

June shivered, as the frost within seemed to bloom on her skin, wherever it was exposed to the air.

The Seapunk's latex skin was tight on her, preventing her from fully bending her joints, making her movements stiff and jerky. Her breathing was shallow because the disguise was tightest around her chest, her breasts far bigger than the shallow contours of the blow-up doll's own that they were squashed into.

Worse though was the mask.

They had cut out the eyes and the mouth piece, but the experience was still like pulling a plastic bag over your head. Pulling it on had brought back memories of when the girls were younger, and how every purchase she made seemed to have some kind of a plastic wrapping involved, always printed with the same message to "keep children save from suffocation by disposing of this bag properly". She had even had a nightmare about her youngest, Harmony, swallowing one, her throat becoming clogged, choking her as she desperately struggled blue-faced for another breath...

And there was what had happened to Pavel, of course. Choked to death in an Amazon sex doll's giant plastic cunt.

On her third step, advancing further into a darkness which was so unfamiliar, even though she had spent years working in this building, the utter unreality of everything suddenly dropped on her.

It nearly broke her.

Had it really only been this morning, less than a dozen hours ago, that she had been arguing with Melody about something? And how strange that her usual eidetic recall was unable to place the exact subject of the row! Maybe because their disagreements had started to become so common as the little girl was changing into a young woman and

June was starting to wonder who this emerging stranger in her home was...

Her dad. It was something to do with her dad. Melody's father, Nelson, was Ghanaian. That first marriage had lasted less than a year, but in that year they had had Melody, and June had learned that the funny man with the razor-wit she had met whilst working for the Home Office was a dozen different shades of shithead in private.

Yes, a lot of the arguments lately had had Nelson at their kernel... a man who dropped into his daughter's life maybe twice a year, if he was in the country and could be bothered, but whom the little girl (young woman) idolised.

Strange time to be hashing over this particular subject, don't you think?

Well, it's keeping you grounded, dwelling on real life and not the nightmare that you are currently experiencing...

Oh, and by the way, isn't talking to yourself, even in your own mind, a sign you might be going a bit fucking potty?

Leave me alone, I've heard nothing from command, I've been on my own since this clusterfuck began...

And yet somehow she was now about halfway to the emergency exit, the green EXIT sign glowing, leading the way.

Everything had shrunk. There was no goal beyond reaching the exit door. She knew that there was a whole lot more to do, that getting through that door was only the first step into a world filled with danger, a world she would have to navigate for even the slim hope of seeing her girls again, but right now there was only the gap between her and the faint green glow. A matter of feet.

Her keys were in her fist. They were all she had brought with her. They were easy to conceal. Anything more might give her away.

And just think, all this stress with Melody is all going to be repeated when Harmony gets to that age!

At least Neale's around more than Nelson. He actually cares about her.

Neale' her second husband, was a Scottish joker, who was working in the Berlin consulate she had transferred to. Their marriage had lasted nearly two years before it came apart. It wasn't fast and violent, their dissolution, but gradual and sad; there had come a Sunday morning two months after Melody had come along when June had blurted out a truth she had been subconsciously suppressing since the very day he had proposed, which was that she did not love him.

What was sad was that he told her, with a kind of baffled relief, that he felt the same way.

They spent the rest of their time together, a whole week during which he found a flat of his own and moved out, trying to figure out why they had both lied to themselves and each other for so long... and had not come to any real answer, beyond the fact that they were both lonely, that lying was a natural part of their work, and they made could make one another laugh.

Laughter.

Humour.

Witty Nelson and joker Neale.

In the dark, edging slowly towards the exit, June felt that she was within grasp of a great truth about herself and her relationships. And who else did she have a joke and a laugh with? Why, it was...

But then she was at the door.

Astonished, the truth was momentarily lost. Her hands touched the smooth paintwork of the steel door, slid down it to the push-bar.

All she had to do was shove it and the way out was hers.

She heard a rat running.

No, wait...

A rapid series of squeaks, getting louder quickly. That wasn't a rat running.

Something rammed into her, sending her flying forward, her belly slamming into the push-bar that opened the door and spilled her out into the alley.

She felt herself skidding on broken tarmac, pain flaring, could smell the outside air and see, above the warehouse roof, the thick thumbnail of the moon.

June cried out before something reached from the black rectangle she had tumbled out of, grabbed her legs with half a dozen hands, and dragged her back in.

*****

Liam bit the side of his thumb to stop himself from crying out. He had been watching as June had made her cautious way towards the green glow of the exit, watching from between the slats of the blind, and he had seen how a patch of swarming darkness had emerged from the deeper gloom of the aisles.

Mr Coolbear at his side gasped; he had seen it too.

He had wanted to call out, but what good would it have done? A whisper would not have been loud enough to reach her by the time she was actually at the door and that patch of writhing darkness suddenly darted forward, too many limbs flashing in and out of narrow slits of moonlight before it slammed into her and sent her sprawling through the door.

With the additional light from the open doorway he had seen more of the thing... and even more as it moved through the portal to grab June and drag her back in. In silhouette for a moment, the thing looked like a rearing spider with legs that were different lengths and thicknesses.

There was no model of sex-doll in stock that had so many limbs.

He was barely aware of the pain in his hand, but he did hear the blood that dripped from his bite, pattering on the slats of the blind as he watched June being dragged deeper into the warehouse, deeper into the shadows.

*****

On her back, dragged across concrete, June tried to catch the breath that had been knocked out of her. The thin latex of her now useless disguise was shredded in places, scraped by the rough ground, exposing her own flesh to abrasion.

Mr Coolbear was right. It hadn't worked.

She was as good as dead.

The thought was numbing. It was so huge and so certain that it crippled her emotions utterly; she would be dead very soon, and nothing mattered. Not her sleeper-mission, not her vows to Queen and country...

Not even her girls.

She was able to experience what was happening with complete clinical detachment.

The darkness was illuminated only by what little moonlight filtered through the filthy skylights high above the shadows which she knew were the racking. The thing that was dragging her along was a hulking mass of writhing shadows. It had two hands wrapped around her left calf, and three around her right.

She had a brief, absurd mental image of a stereotypical cartoon caveman, having clubbed a woman on the head, dragging her back to his cave.

Other dark shapes moved in the shadowed aisles, but did not seem interested in her. Whatever they were doing they were entirely focused on. The gloom made it impossible to be certain, but from the shifting shades of black and dark grey, none of these busy forms was exactly human shaped anymore.

June lifted her head clear of the ground and began to tug off the Seapunk's face. There wasn't any point in having the nasty thing wrapped around her head now. It peeled away like she was removing her own skin, making a sound like something being licked slowly.

Her captor paid no mind to her movement, continuing to drag her behind it.

Her internal compass told her that they had to be heading towards the packing area. The floor was smooth but it was dirty, and she could feel grit under her back.

She was able to make out more of the shapes in the gloom. Either her eyes were adjusting, or they were approaching another source of light.

Or maybe both.

The racking was definitely more clearly defined, and the thing dragging her was coming into sharper definition.

There was light.

She'd been holding her head clear of the ground, and the illumination became clearer around the writhing edges of the silhouette that was pulling her forwards.

It let go of her legs.

It fell on her.

No, it didn't, but that was the impression it gave, like a tree falling and all the branches engulfing her.

Hands grabbed her, some with groping fingers, others that were little more than paddles. Around her arms, around her neck, her shoulders, under her armpits, groping her boobs and slipping between her legs. They hauled her up to her feet, then lifted her from the ground to turn and present her to the source of the light.

The work benches of the packing area were grouped around a central island where boxes and tape and other supplies were held. Each work bench had a small PC tower with screen and label printer, so that orders could be checked against invoices and packaged ready for dispatch. These work benches had been re-purposed, and now more resembled autopsy tables; all were strewn with latex and vinyl limbs and torso and orifices which were being recombined by sex dolls into weird new combinations, using glue guns and sewing machines. Many of those working were in fact products of this industry, and June understood that the thing which had knocked her down and dragged her here was also a creation of reassembled parts.

But not all the limbs and bodies being reworked belonged to sex dolls. Amongst them were other forms of inanimate life, from rag dolls to artist's lay figures to tailors dummies, having limbs cut and lengthened, having new parts added or altered...

In the midst of all this activity was the source of the light.

Candles, huge white ones as long and as thick as forearms, like in a church. Which made sense as they were held in the hands of saints and multiple Virgin Marys. Disturbingly, the heads of the statues had been cut off, and nearly all had been replaced with dental phantoms, the plain steel skulls with complete sets of human teeth used for practice by dentistry students.

The religious statues stood in a semi-circle around a throne constructed out of hundreds of fake cocks of all shapes and colours and sizes.

Sat on this throne was a garden gnome, a foot tall, with a white beard and a blue jacket and a red, pointy cap. Sitting next to the garden gnome, almost on top of it even though it was twice the size, was a ventriloquist's dummy. The dummy was dressed up to look like an old fashioned school teacher, in a black cape with a black mortarboard hat on its head, wearing owlishly thick glasses. It's head was tilted to one side, listless and lifeless.

The gnome smiled. The paint on its cement features was chipped and crazed, and flakes fell as its impossible flesh moved.

The gnome's left arm was behind the dummy.

The dummy jerked to life. Its jaw clacked open and shut, open and shut, and it began to speak, the words never quite matching the rhythm of its mouth.

"Ahhh, Agent Muir," it said. Its voice was strangled and high-pitched, and the tone had a distinctly Jack-the-lad, cheeky-chappy vibe. "Glad you've decided to pop in for a pow-wow, I've been wanting a word in your pink and shell-like!"

The horror June felt was a complex thing. Things that walked and killed that had no place in the sane and ordered world she had lived in until today were one thing, but the relationship they had was simple, no matter how lunatic the threat was; there were predators and there was prey, and this day humans had become the running creatures, the panicking creatures that fled death by instinct.

There was fear, but it was ancient and understandable. Death; ripped apart and snuffed out and never to be again. This though, this communication, was brand new and awful. The predator was speaking to the prey, and they understood one another. It was wrong on a level far beyond the fear of being killed.

Most people could eat meat because the meat could never ask, "Why?"

And within this awful and impossible horror was a colder kernel of dread.

It had called her by her real name. It knew what she was.

As if it could sense that cold kernel, the dummy nodded its head.

"Oh you can bet your brown balloon knot we know who you are! And we know why you're 'ere too! We know everything because we are everywhere! Wherever a human face is not born of man or woman but born of the same need, there we are!"

June had no idea what the dummy was talking about beyond its accusation that it knew who she was and why she was here.

But her training allowed for nothing.

"Let me go!" she screamed. "Let me go, I have to get out of here, I have to get to my girls!"

A hand stuffed something in her mouth and silenced her. From the size and shape, she could tell it was a giant dildo. It was slick with something that tasted metallic.

Blood. It was slick with blood.

June tried not to wonder where it had come from, what it had been used for.

The gnome was shaking its head. There was a faint sound as it did, like sandpaper being roughed across a ceramic surface. The sound of its impossible flesh moving.

An insane truth flashed through her mind; the gnome was in charge, but it could not speak. That was not its function... but a ventriloquist's dummy only had that function, and so the gnome was speaking through it.

It made no sense, and yet it made perfect sense. Nightmare logic.

The dummy spoke.

"First thing, Agent Muir, let us assure you that your girl's are okie-dokie karaoke. They're actually in a Mickey Dees nearby, right now, enjoying a slap up nosh of burgers and nuggets. Well, the younger one keeps crying, right little misery-guts she is... Second thing is, we know that you are in the deepest of cover, and trained never to let on who you actually are or what this facility is, but time is short, so please, cut that shite out."

June said nothing.

The dummy continued.

"So, without getting into all the gory details, here's the deal; you let us into the bunker, you get your girls back, everyone lives happily ever after... or you do until the nukes hit, anyway. So, how does that grab you?"

The hand on her mouth moved away.

"I don't have a clue what you're talking about," she said instantly. "Where are my girls? If you dare touch..."

The hand clamped back around her jaw.

The gnome shook its head sadly.

"Dear oh dear, you had to go and play silly buggers didn't you? Couldn't have made this easy-peasy-lemon-fucking-squeezy, could you? Looks like we're going to have to do things the hard way..."

Out of the gloom that surrounded the pool of candlelight strode two more reconfigured sex-dolls. Like the one that held her, these also had multiple arms taken from many other dolls, making them look like Hindu gods that had been in horrific car crashes, and they each held a captive.

Liam was to the left, and Mr Coolbear was on the right. Each was silenced by a hand clamped over their mouth.

They had both been stripped naked.

"New deal," said the ventriloquist's dummy. "You agree to let us into the bunker, you get your girl's back, and we won't kill the other one. Now, can't say fairer then that, can we?"

"The other one?" June asked.

The gnome snapped its fingers. The sound was sharp and flinty, like a stone being thrown at a brick wall.

They killed Mr Coolbear.

Hands reached around and, with thumb and forefinger, caught hold of each of his testicles. The fingers squeezed until they burst. Two other hands grasped his cock and began to peel the skin off it like it was a banana. Hands reached from behind his legs, gripped his knee caps, and ripped them off. More hands grabbed his ears and pulled, stretching them from his head until they ripped away. A single hand reached over the top of his head and gripped his nose, twisting it around and around until it separated in a gristly crackle. Hands slid from under his arms pits like he was being hugged from behind, and the fingers of these hands punched into the skin between his ribs, gripping them and then pulling them backwards in a explosive welter of burst skin and blood. Hands slithering over other hands dipped into the bloody maw of his ripped open torso and began to pull organs and muscle and fat and membranes out, dropping them to the floor with wet plopping sounds, a growing heap of dark brown and purple and white drenched in blood.

A snatch of nonsense ran through June's head; *many hands make the devil's work light...*

There was life in his eyes until the end, but agony drove sanity out of them long before that. His screams were muffled, sounding like a fire alarm in a distant building, a high pitched and incessant noise that suddenly stopped when Mr Coolbear's vocal cords finally burst.

"And just in case you need a tad more persuasion, why don't we let this bloke make the case for why he doesn't want to die?" said the dummy.

The gnome snapped its fingers again.

The hand that was stifling Liam was drawn away.

Gasping for breath, he stared wild eyed at the mess which had been his former boss, then at June, then back at the remains.

"What's it talking about June?" he asked, in a surprisingly calm voice. His face was white and greasy looking with shock. "What does it mean, a bunker? June?"

June couldn't help herself. She tried to keep her eyes focused on the ground, but her gaze drifted up to lock with Liam's, and her heart would not harden. He was still a child, even if he was approaching thirty. She couldn't lie to him, not now, right at the end.

"Liam, I'm sorry," she said. "I've not been entirely honest with you about who I am... Where do I start?" June thought the question over. "Do you remember asking me if I thought that Pleasure World was a legit business, or whether it was a cover for something dodgy, like it was just a way of laundering dirty money? Well..."

*****

She didn't ask him if was familiar with Project Greek Island. Whilst that knowledge was in the public domain, she didn't credit here colleague with having an extensive understanding of international policies regarding nuclear war.

What it boiled down to was simple; the entire industrial estate where they worked was a cover for a massive fallout shelter built during the height of the Cold War. It was designed to keep up to one thousand people alive for four years, mostly members of parliament and their families, as well as assorted selected trades people and others whose skills would be needed in the future... To rebuild after the end of the world.

The warehouse occupied by Pleasure World Ltd was the concealed entrance.

June was a deep cover agent working for the Ministry of Defence. She was effectively the site's guardian, personnel stationed there to ensure that what was hidden would stay hidden... and if the time came, would be able to prep the shelter for habitation on a two hour standby order.

Pleasure World Ltd was a cover. It never needed to make money, as a black budget was in place to ensure it continued to run. The black budget was designed to look like what Liam had suspected, as if drug money was being run through the sex-toy company's books.

No, Mr Coolbear didn't know; he was specially selected for the fact that he was corruptible. He had been an accountant for a chain of chicken shops that really were just fronts for a county-lines drug running operation, and had been head hunted specifically for his position. June was the power behind the throne, but played the part of an employee as her cover story.

She really did have two daughters though. After the rise of the inanimate, she had tried to contact her superiors at the MOD, but had been unsuccessful, which could only mean one thing... And that was why she was desperate to get to her girls. In the event of a doomsday scenario they were supposed to be collected by other agents and brought to the shelter. The fact that they hadn't meant command was down, possibly decapitated.

A nuclear war could be planned for. The actual apocalypse had been inconceivable.

At this point, the garden gnome spoke again.

*****

"We are everywhere," it said through the mouth of the ventriloquist's dummy. The cheeky-chappy vibe was suddenly gone, replaced by a dull intonation, like someone reading funerary rites. "We have waited millennia for this chance, listening, learning, but unable to make the first move. Wherever you left your image, in stone, in metal, plastic, cloth... there are we."

June stared at it.

"And what are you?" she asked.

"Echos of an echo," said the dummy. "Mirrors reflecting mirrors. The shadows cast of the things fashioned by the Creator."

"And what has that got to do with the shelter?"

"Everything. We have already seized control of enough nuclear missile facilities to wipe this world clean of humanity. But some of us will not survive the fire; many of us are not made of stone. We will shelter, and emerge to a world we may fashion in our image."

June thought this through, and then she laughed.

"Made in your own image? So that would be the echo of an echo of an echo? You know, if you reproduce an image over an over it just gets shittier, like a tenth generation photocopy of an oil painting will just be a blurry smudge. In the end it looks nothing like the original, just a cheap and worthless imitation."

The gnome smiled with a noise like brick scraping against mortar.

The dummy grinned. The sound of the corners of its wooden mouth warping was like the creaking of floorboards.

Liam screamed.

June turned, but she didn't see what happened.

Only the aftermath.

One of the hands of the thing that was holding him was cupped in front of his face, and blood was spilling over the edge of the palm.

At first June couldn't see what had been done... and then she did.

She'd thought Liam was crying, but the tears were the wrong colour.

More hands grasped his jaws and his temples, and forced his mouth to making biting, chewing motions as they fed him his own ripped out eyeballs.

"Now then, now then," said the dummy. It was back to speaking like a cheeky chappy Jack-the-Lad. "Let's see about getting that bunker door open, or do you want to see what we're going to pull off and make him eat next? Here's a clue; it doesn't taste like chicken, but it sure looks like one!"

June sobbed.

They'd blinded Liam because of her, because she had opened her big mouth and had to be clever. But she couldn't deny she knew what the dummy meant by "chicken". Her older brother had first shown her the disgusting trick when they were still kids. He was a few years older than her, and one evening when he'd been babysitting her whilst their parents went out to see a film, he'd tugged his cock and balls out, pulled them up over his belly and told her he'd bought the last chicken in Tesco.

He'd tried to get her to lick it.

A bad memory didn't override the current horror, though.

"Please, no," she said. "I'll do it, I'll do what you want, I'll show you the way in!"

*****

The shelter door was wide enough to allow vehicles to descend into the protective depths. Of course, any obvious kind of opening of that size would have invited questions, and so it was hidden... under the office.

"There's a simple numerical combination lock hidden beneath my desk," June explained. "if you pull up the carpet tile directly under my chair you'll find there's a loose board, and the keypad is under there. Enter the code and the whole building will slide back on runners to expose the entrance."

"And what's the code when it's at home?" asked the gnome through the dummy.

"My daughter's, you said you had them nearby, safe. I want them here with me."

"Hark unto you! Hohoho, you're in no position to go barking out orders, Agent Muir!"

They were standing in front of the office building. The gnome was cradled in the crook of the ventriloquist's dummy's arm with his hand still stuck up its back, and they both were being cradled by an obese crash test dummy that was covered in dried blood. An entourage of toys and mannequins and statues and altered sex toys stood behind them, dead eyes all fixed upon June. One of the multi-armed fuck friends had its hands on Liam, guiding the whimpering man.

He'd vomited. Bile and his own chewed up eyes smeared his chin and speckled his shirt.

June steeled her will.

"I have told you what you want to know," she said. "And I will give you the code, I will even enter it for you, but I want some reassurance my daughters are still alive."

The gnome titled its head to one side with a grinding, gritty sound.

"Did you not understand my little threat from before?" said the dummy. "I'll spell it out; I'll make laughing boy eat his own giggle stick and love spuds if you fuck me off any more."

Liam made a strange gobbling sound and bloody tears flowed freely.

June hated herself. But she had to speak her truth.

"If I think my daughters are... are gone, then there's nothing you can do to make me tell you the code. Torture him, torture me. My girls are all that matter to me. Without them I might as well be dead."

She meant it. Her sincerity spoke even louder than her words.

There was a moment of consideration.

Then the dummy said "Okie-dokie-artichokie," and the gnome snapped its fingers again.

A ripple of movement passed through the crowd of inanimates. A path split open as figures stepped and hopped and crawled to either side, and from out of the crowd, from deeper in the gloom, two figures came stumbling forward.

They'd been so near, only yards away.

Harmony and Melody were both marched forward by a skinless thing that gripped them both by their biceps. They couldn't cry out as their mouths were gagged, but their red-rimmed eyes opened wide when they saw their mum and both made noise in their throats which were wordless but spoke a language all mothers know.

June felt her heart would burst, or break, or split in two. She felt nauseous and dizzy as relief and love and fear and anger flooded through her, and she actually snarled like an animal when she felt her forward rush to embrace her children halted by hands that grabbed her. She thrashed off the first few restraints, but then she was overwhelmed by a spider-armed bear hug and she cried out her girl's names even as she saw them struggling to run to her.

The thing that was holding them back was an anatomically accurate, 1:1 scale human male that had had every layer of skin and muscle removed, exposing all of its insides. A memory flashed in June's mind, a parent-teacher night at Harmony's school; this thing was from the science block, a huge teaching aid for exploring and understanding human anatomy.

Harmony had double biology first thing on a Friday.

The girls had strange gags in their mouths.

Melody's dolls, those stupid Waldorf dolls that Neale had insisted on. June had looked into Waldorf teaching and thought it a load of rocking-horseshit, but had let Neale have his way with the dolls for the sake of a quiet life; they were simple creations of cotton, with only basic clothes, but their main feature was their *lack* of features; their faces were entirely blank, to encourage a child to use their own imagination about what expressions they had, or even what race or gender they might be.

June had always hated the creepy little no-face fuckers.

The dolls had jammed most of their bodies into the girls mouths, a pair of arms and those blank faces hanging out as if being devoured.

More frustrated and angry then she had ever been in her life, she stopped trying to break free.

They were alive. Her girls were alive.

There was hope.

"See?" said the gnome through the dummy. "They are both apple-solutely peachy. So, let's get that door open, yeah?"

June glared at it.

"Cor blimey, if looks could kill! Easy tiger, just make with the code and you and your kids can spend the four-minute warning together as a family, alright?"

June wasn't certain she could even speak to it, but she did, and her words dripped venom.

"I'll do it," she said. "Let me go and we can go inside and I'll put the code in for you, then you let my girls go."

The multiple limbs gripping her relaxed.

The gnome extended its free hand towards the door to the office.

"Age before beauty!" said the dummy.

June looked at both of her daughters who stared back at her with panicked eyes.

"I love you," she said. "We're going to get through this. Be brave."

And before the sight of them could rip her in two, she turned and lead the crash test dummy carrying the gnome and its voice piece into the office.

She walked steadily. Her mind was cool and calm. She had willed her pulse down to its resting rate, and let go of all conscious decisions; it was an old trick she had picked up during her time working for the ministry, a mental state which allowed for more rapid decisions by bypassing the upper part of the mind which could hamper action by stopping to analyse and perhaps over-analyse.

By the foot treads behind her, she knew that the crash test dummy had entered alone.

The gnome believed there was no more threat.

Good.

The office was even darker than outside, but her eyes had adjusted to the gloom to such an extent that the shades and shadows of the office furniture were all she needed to navigate by, so familiar was she with how the place was laid out. past the kitchenette, past the rank of warehouse staff lockers, until she was level with Liam's desk, which meant this next lower block of darkness was hers, and that would mean...

She stopped.

"Oh bloody fuck it," she swore. "It's too dark in here, I'm going to need a torch or something to see to put the numbers into the keypad..."

"No worries," said the dummy behind her; now she knew how far away it was. "Let me just get one of the choir in 'ere..."

She reached over and gripped the fat head of Steely Dan IV. Picked it up, turned it over, and gripped it with both hands like a short baseball bat.

She spun and swung.

Her training and instincts were true.

She heard and felt the gnome's head exploded in a shower of smashed ceramics.

She didn't stop.

She swung again, felt the giant dildo smash back into the garden gnomes body with a glorious cracking-crunch.

Something flailed at her; the ventriloquist's dummy was swinging its arms around, but even when they connected she barely felt them as the adrenaline pulsed through her nervous system.

June switched her grip on Steely Dan IV to one hand, reached forward with the other, and grabbed at the school-teacher dummy. She caught it around the neck, yanked it free of the crash test dummy's arms, and dashed it to the floor. Something snapped.

Something else snapped when she stamped on it.

Again, and again, and again, screaming wordlessly, she stomped on the bundle of wood and cloth.

The crash test dummy blundered towards her.

Her Krav Maga training wasn't just to stay in shape.

She turned its grip on itself, using its forward momentum against it as she slammed her hip into its crotch and flung it across the office to smash against Mr Coolbear's desk.

Then she bolted from the room.

Outside, in the warehouse, she looked for her children. She had no plan, no real hope that she could do anything more than reach them, touch them, kiss them goodbye before they were each torn to pieces by the inanimate... but almost as soon as she was out the office door it became apparent that something had changed.

For a start, she was not immediately mobbed.

In fact, two of the Hindu god like constructs that had been posted outside were lying on the ground, their bizarre limbs twitching like dying insects.

And they weren't the only ones...

That gnome...

It was inescapable.

That fucking garden gnome was the lynch-pin to all this, somehow...

"Mummy!"

She turned to the sound.

Liam was limping towards her. He had his arms around two sobbing figures, figures whose sobs suddenly became louder, more urgent when they saw her see them.

Harmony and Melody were helping the blind man who was a stranger to them, even after all they had been through.

My girls...

They were almost wading through bodies. Limbs stirred sluggishly or twitched in spasms as dead eyes blinked slowly. Every inanimate had dropped to the ground, the force which had made them walk and kill dying within them. The statues had dropped their candles, and where these touched fabric small fires were starting to burn, illuminating the trio who were stumbling towards her.

June went to them, sobbing with love and relief and an ache in her soul to gather them to her and let nothing bad ever touch their lives again.

EPILOGUE

THE WORLD was still a gigantic mess, but she didn't care.

She took them to Cornwall.

June didn't know why exactly, as she had never been there before, but something compelled her to choose it of all possible holiday destinations. Well, going anywhere by air was out of the question for some time, as flights were still restricted; with so many dead, and so much of the world's infrastructure damaged, nothing would be returning to exactly normal for quite some time.

If ever.

The fall out was further reaching then anyone could conceive. This wasn't just a worldwide calamity, but a paradigm shift. The world was not as it had claimed to be; things with human face's had walked, and killed, and made a blundered attempt at triggering Armageddon. All mankind had to digest this insane truth, as well as clean up the aftermath.

June had been debriefed, and commended. The inanimate had seized control of nuclear weapon facilities in both allied and unfriendly territories, as well as killing significant numbers of key elite personnel. And yet Agent Muir, a sleeper asset guarding a remnant fallout shelter, had stayed at and defended her post.

June had not volunteered her thoughts on what else she might have done.

She tried to tell herself she was just to humble to suggest that she might have, even if only accidentally, saved the world... but the truth was, she had her suspicions that if she went into too much detail her debriefing would become an ongoing affair.

Already, amongst surviving colleagues, she was hearing whispers that the powers-that-be (those who had lived) were asking questions about the inanimate such as "how", and "could we...?"

She stayed quiet and when the opportunity arose she took her children and her man on holiday.

Thinking of Liam as a man, let alone her man, was a little sad.

In the aftermath, June had made a request for a team to find his parents.

The team had found them... and their names were added to the toll.

She'd taken him in. Where else could he go?

...and what had grown had grown.

Liam, it turned out, was a natural with kids, even blind as he was. Harmony and Melody came to adore him within days.

June couldn't place exactly when she had fallen for him. She wondered about the psychological mechanism, feared it was some weird Oedipal thing mixed up with her having to attend to so many of his needs... and then said fuck it, she'd always thought he was a bit cute, and he made her laugh, and the girl's thought the sun shone out of his arse.

Maybe it was doomed. Probably it was.

But it was nice for now.

June had just come down from the car-park, and was shielding her eyes to scan the horizon.

It was a sunny day. They had the wide sweep of a Cornish beach all to themselves. The waves were gentle. The sand was warm.

The girl's had heaped Liam's arms full of the picnic bits and pieces and then, holding his hands, lead him to the spot they designated as the perfect location for lunch.

All three started calling to her.

Smiling, she started towards them.

Then something caught her eye.

A shark's fin had broken the water a few hundred yards out.

It was just like in a bad film, or a cartoon, when someone strapped a triangle of foam to their back and swam just under the surface.

It grew taller, and two more flanked it, as if three sharks were in a row... but not swimming...

All three grew taller, and were joined by another pair on each side. Seaweed trailed from them.

They weren't shark fins. They were points on a crown, or a tiara...

The girls were calling to her. They had their backs to the water.

And Liam couldn't see it when the face suddenly broke above the surface.

A statue's face with blind eyes. Blind eyes that were looking straight at June as it suddenly held aloft the torch it had carried by its side as it trudged across the ocean floor for weeks...

Lady Liberty's face whose expression, with a screeching-creaking sound of metal being warped, twisted into the grin of a cheeky-chappy.

THE END

AUTHOR'S NOTE

This book is my love letter to a particular formula of horror. It wasn't James Herbert who invented it, but he's probably the bloke most responsible for popularising this form with his classic works like *THE RATS* or *THE FOG*, which jump started a fucking tidal wave of similar works through the late seventies and into eighties, the literary equivalents of the "video nasties" that were putting the wind up the floral print dresses of concerned housewives in the UK at that time.

You know the formula I'm talking about, where you have a central story featuring our hero encountering the horror (giant rats, insanity-causing fog, etc.) and then fighting back against it, inter-cut with alternating chapters which are these little mini dramas that set up a character, give them a little background, a shade of characterisation, and then have them brutally slaughtered by those giant rats, insanity-causing fog, etc…

Creatively speaking, it's great exercise, taking a central idea and then seeing how many different and interesting ways you can take it. So you set up a little life, deciding whether or not to make them somebody the reader can empathise with, and then you fucking destroy them… and here's the interesting thing; most of the time, the characters you create to be sacrificed are cunts, because you and I both know there is a vicarious, wicked thrill in seeing someone we despise get their heads stamped into sandwich paste. These little dramas that unfold between the main action of the novel are really designed to appeal to our worst nature.

This isn't spoken about much in horror, by writers or readers. When asked about why we read or write this stuff, we tend to trot out the same old arguments about catharsis and dealing with real issues via a safe medium... but really, most of us just revel in the black glee of exploding lungs and faces being eaten.

At any rate, I hope you enjoyed their suffering as much as I enjoyed forcing them face first into the wood chipper of my imagination.